Skills To Kill
A Steve Dane Thriller

Brian Drake

WOLFPACK PUBLISHING
— EST 2013 —

WOLFPACK
PUBLISHING
— EST 2013 —

The characters and events portrayed in this book are fictitious. Any
similarity to real persons, living or dead, is coincidental and not
intended by the author.

Text copyright © 2021 (As Revised) Brian Drake

Published by Wolfpack Publishing
5130 S. Fort Apache Road, 215-380
Las Vegas, NV 89148

Paperback IBSN 978-1-64734-642-3
eBook ISBN 978-1-64734-641-6

Skills To Kill

For Sarah.

Also for Jerry Ahern. Thanks for writing.

Part I:
The Private Vendetta

Chapter One

It was the sharpest order Steve Dane had ever received:

"Shoot him!"

Dane laughed and shifted in the bed. The accordion down the hall continued blaring. Nina rolled away from him and pulled the covers over her.

Male and female laughter mingled with the noise. The party had been going on since midnight.

"Laugh all you want," she said. "You won't get any of my goodies until that man is dead." Her words were dusted with a soft Russian accent.

Dane said, "Other than the noise, it's a nice hotel, right?"

"It is not. I get to pick next time."

"This is one of the nicest hotels in Italy. This is what you wanted."

"Next time we'll go to Geneva."

The downstairs staff had acknowledged receiving many complaints, but they were powerless to help. The accordion player was a pop star, whose name Dane had forgotten, who had lots and lots of money that he spent at the hotel and surrounding establishments, and they were not going to disturb him lest he start breaking things and decide to spend his lots and lots of money elsewhere.

"It's too late for polka," Dane had told them. "It's the wrong *century* for polka."

The appeal had been ignored.

This was no way to start a vacation.

Dane drifted off to sleep and started to snore. He jerked awake for a moment when Nina punched him in the arm.

Dane rose before Nina, who lay on her stomach, arm dangling over the side of the bed. Her snoring sounded like a chain saw stuck in a log. After a hot shower, he scraped whiskers off his face and pulled from the closet a set of clothes he'd had the hotel dry-clean and press the day before.

The long-sleeved Sedona Silk shirt with pearl buttons fit perfectly, covering the warped and puckered flesh on his right arm. Years ago, while on a CIA assignment in Central America, the Blackhawk helicopter used by Dane and his team crashed in the jungle. The ruptured fuel tanks splashed gasoline onto his clothes and the clothes of a friend trapped in the wreckage. Dane pulled his friend out before the chopper exploded, but the flames still reached them, igniting their fuel-soaked fatigues, and they went up like Roman candles. Dane hit the dirt and rolled back and forth like a madman and put the fire out. He'd been lucky. Only his right arm, part of his side and chest, and a portion of his right leg had been affected. His friend Len Lukavina had not been so lucky.

To Dane the scars had become a symbol with its own motto: *"You've survived the worst. Everything else is easy."*

But the scars also symbolized a darker truth: *"You are not invincible."*

He strictly wore long-sleeved shirts in a futile effort to

hide the damage and deny what had happened. He knew he was fooling himself, but he also couldn't break the habit.

After cutting loose from the CIA, Dane formed a mercenary unit called the 30-30 Battalion. A skirmish in South Africa netted him control of a diamond mine turning out enough stones to keep him solvent the rest of his life, and he disbanded the unit. It was time to fight the battles he wanted, to bring a fight to the predators who sought to exploit the defenseless who had nobody to turn to. Idealistic, yes, he could afford to be idealistic. And he could afford the luxurious lifestyle that came with such independence.

Plenty of action, plenty of rough spots, and he'd always come out on top. But it hadn't been his choice to take off on his own. The decision was made for him the day his father shot himself after being accused of treason, a charge his son knew wasn't true. Dane tried his best but couldn't uncover evidence to the contrary. Then he almost died in a helicopter fire. That was it for him. He took off for the wild pastures of the world and left home behind.

He ran a hand over the close-cropped black fuzz atop his head and decided that another haircut was due soon. At least the flames hadn't reached that spot, the one area he couldn't conceal.

He pulled on a pair of Mick Marten black slacks, fastening the leather belt. He slipped on the spit-shined black leather shoes, with steel toes, next.

He left the bedroom for the suite's living room and sat on the brown leather couch, which matched the dark walls and cabinetry. Both rooms of the suite were in a combination of light brown and off-white that only the Italians could pull off. He scanned news headlines on his phone.

The world, he read, was in its usual state of chaos. Every now and then he glanced at the bedroom, where Nina was still snoring. About an hour later when he finished reading, he flung the covers off and smacked her plump behind. She awoke with a jolt mid-snore and cussed him up one side and down the other in a string of rapid Russian.

She trudged into the bathroom while Dane stepped out on the deck and lit a Glandon Family cigar. The hot tub off to the right was cold now, the water still, and he smiled at the memory of their quiet romp in the water the previous night. The canopy above blocked the bright sun, and the wooden deck and brass railing reminded him of being on a cruise ship, though he tried to avoid those as much as possible. He listened to the chirping birds and the breeze and Nina's splashing in the shower.

She had once been a highly decorated agent with the Russian FSB. She and Dane met when Dane was in Europe investigating the possibility that a pair of Anastasia's jewels had shown up on the black market. The "possibility" had been a ruse, the jewels nothing but a pair of really good fakes, but as Dane sought the items for his own profit and Nina for her country's history, their genuine chemistry assured both that they would soon pledge their remaining days to each other.

Nina remained angry through breakfast. They sat in a back corner of the hotel coffee shop munching brioche and drinking cappuccino. They were in Mestre, Italy, about twenty minutes from Venice via the Freedom Bridge.

Nina swallowed the last bite of her roll while Dane spread jam on his. The window next to them looked out on a busy street; Dane sat with his back to the wall, eyeing everyone who entered. One never knew where a snake might show up, so it was best to look under every rock.

Another brioche waited on his plate. Nina reached across the table, broke the roll in half, and ate it. Crumbs landed on her green sweater.

"Keep that up and you'll get fat," he said.

"What do you care? This body is off-limits to you."

"Go all the way or go home," he said, and set the remaining half on her plate.

She bit into the half, her unblinking glare fixed on his face.

Dane laughed again, looking at her. Soft features and big brown eyes disguised the lethality brimming beneath the surface.

Dane had his own hungry and defensive look to him. Ever-alert eyes, a habit of sitting in front of a wall, as he did this morning, but he wasn't afraid of predators, despite those out for his head. The prey sought by other predators, and how he could offer resistance and shelter to those unable to provide their own, occupied his mind.

"This was supposed to be relaxing," she said, "after our work in London."

Their last bit of buccaneering concerned the CEO of a charity who had embezzled funds—nearly all of the funds. They set up quite a con (the plot was Nina's idea), fleeced every dollar from the worm, and returned it to the charity minus a 15-percent commission. And the worm was cooling it in a jail cell. He'd been stupid enough to leave a paper trail of evidence (or had it been fabricated?) that assured conviction.

They had earned a rest.

"Sugar bear," Dane said, "we never rest for very long."

Dane brushed crumb bits off his blue shirt and stood up. Nina gathered her purse, slipped on a pair of sunglasses and refused Dane's outstretched arm.

"Now you're being silly," he said.

"We'll start our tour looking at museums," she said.

"Why don't you just shoot *me* instead?"

He paid the check and they went outside. The morning air was spiced with the crisp scent of the sea just a few miles away.

They waited at the curb until a gray Jaguar F-Type swung around the corner. A uniformed valet hopped out and handed Dane the keys in exchange for a large tip.

A striking young woman also at the curb watched the street. Long black hair stretched down her back; she wore a pink sweater, checkered skirt and black leather stilettos. Quite the mod ensemble.

Nina jabbed Dane's side. "She's not even finished growing yet."

Dane put his hand to Nina's cheek and planted a kiss on her lips. "You exhaust me."

The young woman screamed.

When a black car pulled up and the back door opened, the girl looked inside and started to say something but cut the words off. She turned and ran. From the other side, a suited man jumped out and grabbed her. He pinned her arms back and shoved her into the car. She struck her head on the edge of the roof, and the blow chopped off further protest. The suited man slammed the door.

Other pedestrians gawked.

Steve Dane launched into action.

Chapter Two

Dane tackled the suited man. He soon felt the power behind the man's muscles when the man kicked Dane away. Both scrambled to their feet, and the suited man struck with a series of kicks and punches. Dane deflected some of the blows, but others landed, each sending a shock of pain through his body. Dane struck the man's jaw. The man recoiled but shifted into a backspin kick that put Dane on the ground. The suited man ran back into the car, and the car took off into traffic.

Dane pushed himself to his feet and ran to the Jag. Nina shouted, "Hey!" Dane left a cloud of smoke in his wake. He weaved through traffic, honking the horn, keeping the black car in sight.

A second black car closed quickly on his rear and tapped the bumper. The Jag surged forward a little. Dane steered it straight. The backup car approached again. Dane swung into the next lane.

Dane glanced over at the driver and passenger, two tough-looking thugs with thick hair. The driver slammed the side of his vehicle into the passenger side of Dane's

Jag. Metal crunched. The side glass split into a string of spider cracks.

Dane's car plowed across the median. Oncoming traffic swerved. Dane wrenched the car back to the correct side of the road. The backup car struck him again, this time on the front panel, and Dane hit the brakes, falling back. He sped up again, but the second car's brake lights flared. Dane slammed his own but the Jag collided anyway. More metal crunched. Smoking rubber and the stink of burning brakes filled the cabin. The smash made the seatbelt strain against his body. The strap bit into his neck. He relaxed against the seat, wincing. Brakes behind him screeched, but nobody else crashed into him. Dane watched both black cars speed away.

He jumped out of the car to check the damage. The collision had caved in the front end. The car behind him sat at a diagonal angle, and out the corner of one eye Dane saw a man get out. Another man, this one older, sat in the back seat of the car. Nina was in the back seat with him. The older man was holding a gun to Nina's head.

"Come with me," the young man said. "Now."

The car was a blue four-door Mercedes. At least the leather seats felt like a couch, soft and comfy, and the driver had no problem keeping the interior climate at a cool 73 degrees, according to the dashboard readout.

Dane and Nina settled back for the ride. They were squished next to each other, with the older man and his never wavering automatic against the other door.

Dane said, "You okay?"

"Not a mark. These nice men asked me to accompany them a few moments after you left."

Dane pulled at the torn fabric of his shirt. "Guess this

one's getting tossed."

"You can afford it."

"Hey, Pops," Dane said to the older man, "you can put the gun away."

The older man, unblinking, did not respond.

Dane turned to the driver. "Junior, tell Pops to put the gun away. We aren't going anywhere."

Junior laughed a little.

"I think," Nina said, "that he thinks you're some sort of tough guy." She called out, "He's not. He's soft and mealy. He won't even shoot a stupid accordion player."

"I am not soft," Dane said. "I'm hard-boiled. I'm also two-fisted."

"You're no Spetsnaz," Nina said.

"Stop talking," Junior snapped.

Dane patted Nina's leg and straightened his cuffs to cover any exposed skin.

Junior left the city limits. They passed farms and large homes. Further in the distance, more green countryside awaited, apparently unclaimed by the locals. A long drive through the region would make a nice afternoon activity, Dane decided, as long as they survived their present trip.

But if the two palookas had meant to kill them, they would have been dead already.

Nina sat with her hands in her lap. Her purse sat between them. She made eye contact with Dane and dropped her eyes to the purse, and then looked back at Dane and blinked twice. The thugs had not searched her purse. Minus ten points for Pops and Junior. They must have grabbed her as soon as he took off after the kidnappers. Dane would have expected Pops to have the attention to detail his kid apparently lacked.

The car turned into a circular driveway and stopped in

front of a house, one story, made of marble and stone, a large formal garden on one side, a vineyard on the other. The front double doors looked like solid oak.

"Nice," Nina said as she eyed the vineyard. "This day may improve yet."

Pops and Junior escorted Dane and Nina inside and into a sitting room, where a large man occupied a motorized wheelchair. Both of the man's legs stopped at the knees.

The man's legs were gone but his upper body was solid. Chiseled jaw, prominent cheekbones, dark eyes. He examined Dane and Nina. He had long ago reached the other side of sixty, but plenty of life burned in his eyes.

The man's face registered in Dane's mental mug file, and he had a sinking feeling that the man seated before him was supposed to be dead.

"Good morning," the man said. "My name is Dominico Russo." He turned to the escorts. "Leave us," he ordered. Junior and Pops stepped out.

"I thought I recognized you," said Dane.

"You would have disappointed me if you had not, Mr. Dane. It is a pleasure to finally meet you and the beautiful Miss Nina Talikova."

"Care to fill in some blanks?" Nina said.

"Perhaps you can explain, Mr. Dane?"

"Dominico Russo," Dane said. "Big boss in Eastern Europe for La Cosa Nostra. Never served a day of jail time, even as a young man."

Russo smiled. "That would be exaggerating a bit. Go on."

"What else is there? You ran your empire with an iron fist, but somebody thought he could take it from you, and that same somebody blew up your boat. Rumors of your death have floated around for the last fifteen years."

Dominico Russo nodded. "The blast killed my wife and took my legs. There is more to the story than somebody wanting to take my place, but we shall get there in a moment. I quietly retired to this place. I have a small staff, two of which you have met, and they are loyal."

"I bet a certain young lady with long black hair and a thing for leather stilettos means something to you."

"That was my daughter. Please, both of you sit down. You are making me feel like a terrible host. What would you like to drink? I make my own wine here. A merlot. Or would Miss Talikova prefer vodka?"

"Merlot, please," she said. "Bring on those vitamins."

Pops served them at a glass table in the garden. Roses bloomed. Bright sky above. Nina sipped red wine while Dane sipped Maker's Mark mixed with Coke. Dane leaned forward with elbows on the table, while Nina sat back with crossed legs. Her purse remained on her lap.

"How did you know who we were?" Dane said.

"You are not unknown in the world, Mr. Dane. Word of your exploits has gone from one end of the planet to another. I find it amusing some are confused as to whether you are on the good side or the bad."

"What do you think?" Dane said.

"I wouldn't have you here if I thought you were anything like me," Russo said, his face grim.

Dane remained impassive. Nina looked surprised by the answer. Dane decided getting his legs knocked off put some humanity back into Russo's soul. The younger Russo wouldn't have talked like that. Russo was slightly wrong, however. Sometimes Dane *was* just as bad as the dragons he sought to slay, but for the right reasons.

"I pay a man at your hotel to let me know who checks in every day," Russo continued. "I also get copies of lobby photographs. I have that arrangement with every hotel in the city. When my men informed me of what happened in front of the hotel, I made the obvious connection."

"I wish I could have done more," Dane said.

"You had not the equipment or manpower to do anything, Mr. Dane. What you did required a personal sacrifice that nobody, in this day and age, seems willing to demonstrate. I admire your confidence, but it can also be your undoing. I spent a lot of years thinking I was untouchable. Look at what's left of me."

Dane's smile looked weak. You aren't the only one. He said, "What's left of you still seems formidable to me, Mr. Russo."

"You are being kind. But enough of that. I have called you here to finish the job, for which I will pay you a great deal of money. Please. I want my daughter home. I want the person who took her disposed of. I know you are not unwilling to kill if a person deserves death, and the official reputation of the two of you speaks volumes.

"Will you do me this favor? Money is no object. Leila must be found. She is all I"—he stopped, swallowed—"all I have left."

"We wouldn't know where to start," Dane said.

"A place to start," Russo said, "will be the easy part."

Chapter Three

"Leila," Russo said, "has always lived apart from me, especially in my heyday. She does not know where I live. We visit often, but I always go to her. We established these precautions when she was young, because of my enemies, and increased them after the attack on my boat. Leila was in high school when that happened. Somehow, some way, she was summoned to Mestre by note, allegedly signed by me. The note says she was to meet me outside the hotel."

Dane nodded.

"She checked into the hotel this morning before I could intercept her," Russo said. "Here is the note." He produced the piece of folded paper from a side pocket of the wheelchair. "Two others from my staff searched her room while you were in transit."

Dane looked at the note and showed it to Nina. It was nothing special. A handwritten note with a curving signature. On its face, it meant nothing. Dane said so.

"The note may not shed any light on who is behind Leila's abduction," the man in the wheelchair said, "but this other letter does. It arrived before you did, so I assume they delivered it as soon as they had her in the car."

Russo produced the new letter from his shirt pocket. Dane read it. Nina looked over his shoulder. The note demanded that Russo show up at a park later that night. Nobody had signed the bottom.

Dane said, "So this is where they will demand a ransom?"

"I suppose."

"I guess a telephone call was too hard."

Nina said to Russo, "They want you out in the open."

"I cannot go out. Not in my condition. Please go in my place. You are authorized to accept any terms and make any promises you think need to be made."

Dane held up the new note. "May I keep this?"

"Of course."

"You have a bargain, Mr. Russo."

"My friends call me Nico."

Dane smiled. "You may call me Steve."

"And you may call me," Nina said, "*Miss* Talikova."

A loud laugh bubbled up from Dominico Russo's belly. "You remind me of my beloved Stephania, rest her soul."

"There is one more thing, Nico," Dane said. "As your new friend, I have to tell you this."

Russo cocked an eyebrow. "Yes?"

"Show him, baby."

Nina reached into her purse and took out her compact 9mm Smith & Wesson M&P Shield. She placed the black polymer pistol on the table.

"Your men," Dane said, "need a refresher course."

Russo nodded. "I am glad this was a friendly visit."

"One more thing," Nina said. "Why us instead of your organization?"

"Because somebody in the organization," Dane said,

"caused this problem."

Russo nodded. "Correct, Mr. Dane. I do not know who I can trust."

"Pops and Junior?"

"You mean Luigi and Pasquale. They are trustworthy. The others too."

"How do you know for certain?"

"There are some things a man knows, Mr. Dane."

"Is finding the traitor part of our job?" Nina said.

"No," said Russo. "I have my own way of doing that. Of course, if you should learn something"—he smiled—"I know you will do the right thing."

Dane and Nina returned to the hotel and sat in the bar. The waitress delivered Nina's stirred martini and Dane's gimlet. The bartender had gone heavy on the lime juice and substituted vodka for gin, but Dane had long ago accepted the fact that nobody outside of England made a proper gimlet. A proper gimlet, as somebody once said, is half gin and half Rose's Lime Juice and *nothing* else.

"A toast," he said. "To our usual shenanigans. May they convince the gray hairs to bother lesser mortals."

They sat in a far corner with low light. A piano player filled the room with soft music.

Nina said, "Think they'll watch us?"

"Junior and Pops will be too busy keeping an eye on Russo," Dane said. "And I'm not convinced they can handle themselves even if the pizza hits the fan."

"He isn't exactly the kind of person you think should be walking free. Why make the deal?"

"He gave you two bottles of wine," Dane said. "He can't be that bad. Also assume the girl is an innocent bystander. This isn't her battle. She doesn't deserve to be involved."

Nina shrugged and sipped her drink.

"Plus, friends in low places are as important as friends in high places. We may need brother Nico if the cops get uppity."

"We were here on vacation."

"Face it," he said. "We would be lost without any action." Dane checked his watch. "Pretty soon we'll have plenty."

That evening they sat in the restaurant over a big dinner. Like the rest of the hotel, the restaurant was decorated with cabin décor and rustic furnishings. A three-paned cone chandelier hung above the table. Nina found the atmosphere dreary, but it reminded Dane of his grandfather's Montana ranch, which no longer existed, where he had spent many summers as a child.

Dane cut his filet mignon into small pink squares and savored each bite, while Nina munched on grilled salmon covered in a cream sauce. Neither went cheap on liquor and food; life was to be lived and lived at high speed. While the suffering martyrs of the world preached against the evils of red meat, they devoured the "evil" stuff and enjoyed every moment.

"This sauce is the best thing about this meal," she said.

"Are you still pissed at me?"

She cocked an eye at him. "Temporary truce. When do you think the cops will want to see you?" Nina sipped some red wine.

"Now," Dane said, nodding over her shoulder.

The man who entered the dining room had cop written all over him. It wasn't something any member of the law enforcement community could hide. The way they squared their shoulders or scanned a room, all of those little and seemingly insignificant "tells" communicated to somebody like Dane exactly whom he was dealing with. The cop's suit fit his stocky body well, and light shined off of his bald head. He looked just shy of forty.

Dane had placed a third chair at the table and now pushed it out with his foot. "Good evening, officer," he said when the man stopped at the table. "Please have a seat."

The cop frowned at Dane. He remained on his feet a moment. Nina put her fork down and watched him. The cop sat down and smiled at Nina. He turned to Dane.

"Mr. Dane. I am Lazzaro Palermo. I am a detective with—"

"I know."

"I have a few questions about your activities today."

"We took a bus to Venice and spent the day on a gondola," Dane said. "Right, honey?"

"That's right. *Honey.*"

Palermo cleared his throat. "I have ten witnesses who said you engaged in physical combat with a man who shoved a woman into a car, apparently against her will. Who was that man, and why did you get involved?"

"I have no idea," Dane said. "I decided to help because that's what I do."

"You have brought yourself and your companion to the attention of my office, Mr. Dane. How is that productive?"

"You know who I am," Dane said. "You probably spent the afternoon going through a certain Interpol report about me, am I right?"

"You are not wanted in Italy," Palermo said. "I would hate very much to see that change. If you had a disagreement with your confederates—"

Dane laughed. "I had nothing to do with what appears to be a kidnapping, Detective. I tried to stop it. Interpol likes to think that I'm the anti-Christ, but I assure you I am merely a humble servant of the Lord, who finds himself under constant persecution. Like right now."

"Yet you saved a seat for me."

"I'll buy you dinner if you want."

"I'm on duty," Palermo said. "You know nothing?"

"Nothing."

"What had you hoped to accomplish by chasing the vehicle the woman was shoved into?"

Nina jumped in, "Stevie can't resist a damsel in distress."

"Does that description apply to you, Miss Talikova?"

"No," she said. "I only use Stevie for sex. And his money."

"Not necessarily in that order," Dane added. "Is there anything else I can help you with?"

"I spoke with Interpol," Palermo said. "They told me to expect that you will continue to stick your nose where it does not belong. I am going to give you one warning. You had better stay clean in my town."

"And the kidnappers?"

"We have our people working on that."

"Any idea who that the woman is?"

"Enjoy your vacation, Mr. Dane. Make sure it becomes nothing more."

"And if it does?"

"As you Americans say, no more Mr. Nice Guy."

Nina said, "I'm not American. Does any of what you said apply to me?"

The cop smiled at Nina and excused himself. Dane waited for him to clear the entryway. None of the other patrons or staff seemed to notice the visit. He said to Nina, "I guess it's up to you, babe."

"Do you even have to ask?"

"I knew you would say that."

She winked.

Chapter Four

Dane returned to their suite while Nina went to get the new loaner car provided by Russo, a Dodge Charger with a big V8 engine.

From the bottom of his suitcase, Dane withdrew a leather shoulder harness. A stainless steel semi-automatic pistol waited in the compartment. The gun was a Detonics Scoremaster in .45 caliber. He slipped his arms through the harness and secured the straps to his belt. The gun hung under his left armpit. His jacket completely covered the harness, and no bulge showed. Dane watched himself in the mirror as he practiced a few draws; dropping two spare 8-round magazines in each pocket of the jacket, he left the room and joined Nina on the street.

"We'll get there about an hour early," Nina said as she merged into traffic.

"I wish you had a machine gun."

"Forget that," she said. "I should have a rocket launcher."

"But you can't fit one of those in your purse."

"Only because one that big hasn't been made yet."

Dane laughed. "If I ever get killed, you can retire to the

Alps and design one yourself."

"If you ever get killed, darling, I fully intend to die with you."

"Ah ha, you still love me after all."

"Don't push your luck."

The park was one big wide-open space with a few trees. The note ordered Dane to stand by the picnic table. Nina found a place to hide and blended into the shadows. Dane sat on top of the table smoking a Macanudo. He didn't think the meeting would end in a shooting, but the enemy was expecting to see Russo and could have anything in mind.

Dane had smoked the cigar halfway when a car pulled up curbside. He watched a man get out of the back. Before the man shut the door, Dane saw the tip of a cigarette flare inside the car. There was a second man in the back, but he wasn't getting out. The first man shut the door, and Dane watched the second man scoot closer to the window. The driver remained in the car as well. The driver did not turn off the engine.

A light wind rustled the trees. Dane glanced around. No movement in the surrounding shadows.

The man from the car approached the table. His long blonde hair was tied back in a ponytail. He wore the pre-requisite black, but instead of a suit, a sport jacket covered a black sweater. His shoes scraped the paved pathway surrounding the picnic table.

"You aren't Russo," the man said. He stopped a few feet from the table.

"Russo is here by proxy," Dane said. He slipped off the table.

"Pity. This would have gone a whole lot smoother. Who are you?"

"Steve Dane."

The blonde man blinked a few times. "Really. Old Nico had to hire somebody?"

"Good help is hard to find."

"Don't I know it," the man said.

"And you are?"

"Never mind who I am." He reached inside his jacket. Dane had the Detonics .45 aimed at the blonde man's left eye before he withdrew his hand.

Dane said, "Do it slow."

"Relax." The hand came out holding a white envelope. He raised it to eye level. "Terms." The man stretched out his arm, and Dane took the envelope in his free hand.

"Is this all?"

"For now." The blonde man turned and went back to his waiting vehicle. The driver pulled away.

Dane wanted to follow the car. But the opposition had kept a second car in reserve during the kidnapping. Dane figured they had the same playbook in use tonight. There was no reason to take the risk.

Dane put away the .45 and sat again. He opened the envelope and turned the paper so he could read it by the streetlight. A twig snapped behind him, but he ignored it. He said, "Too much noise."

"You don't normally complain," Nina said, emerging from the other side of a nearby tree. She stopped alongside him. "What is that?"

"The oddest terms I have ever seen," he said.

He showed her the one-sentence note: *I want what you can't give.*

It was signed: *The Animal.*

"That's odd," Nina said.

"Where is Miss Talikova?" Dominico Russo said.

"I dropped her off at the hotel," Dane said. He took a seat at the same couch he had sat at during his first visit. Russo wheeled close by. Dane described the meeting and showed Russo the note. Russo read the note, dropped his hand in his lap and lowered his head.

"What does this mean, Nico?"

"Amalio 'The Animal' Milani."

"Former enemy?"

"I shot his brother. He swore revenge. He must have been the one who blew up my boat. How he found me, how he found Leila…" He sighed. "It took him years, but he did."

"I don't think he knows about your condition," Dane said. "They expected you. There was a second man in the car that showed up. He watched me and the representative the whole time. I bet that was Milani. He wanted to watch you read the note and start begging."

Russo shook his head. "What difference does it make?"

"You've told me who," Dane said, "but what else does it mean?"

"I cannot give him back his brother, so he is going to take my daughter."

Dane looked at the man and ran through a few scenarios in his mind. If there was nothing they could give "The Animal" in exchange, they would have to attempt a rescue. Dane frowned once he realized he had nothing to go on. The blonde man had not given his name, nor had Dane seen any distinguishing marks on the blonde man's car. Nina, from where she hid, had not been able to see the car. She'd been watching for an ambush, not taking notes.

"What are you thinking about?"

Dane told him. "I'm not sure what to do." He smiled. "When I was younger, I used to read a lot of Raymond Chandler books. He always said that when his stories slowed down, he'd move things along by having a guy with a gun walk into a room."

Dane turned to watch the doorway, but nobody entered, armed or otherwise.

"Maybe next time," he said.

"I do not understand you," Russo said.

"That's okay, Nico. I don't understand me either." Dane stood and straightened his clothes. "I'll dig up something. I promise."

The man in the wheelchair said, "I believe you will."

Chapter Five

As Dane drove away, he knew of one possibility that he had not shared with Russo. Milani saw him. That meant Russo had muscle that Milani had not been counting on, and thus put his plan in jeopardy. Dane would have to be terminated.

He used his cell to call Nina. She reported that she was in the middle of a hot bath. She also reported that she had killed half a bottle of Russo's wine and was feeling no pain.

"The accordion player is making noise again," she reported.

"I'm expecting some action, so I need you to—"

"Did you hear me? I said the *accordion player*—"

"I *get* it, darling. Your goodies are currently unavailable. But we have a girl to rescue," he said. "Keep your gun handy. I'll knock three times before I come in."

"What if in my stupor I suspect you're a bad guy and shoot you?"

"Honey, in the condition you're in, I bet you can't see straight."

"You are so smart!"

He ended the call with a curse as a pair of headlights

grew bright in his rearview mirror. That was fast. Dane un-buttoned his jacket for easy access to his artillery. He sped up. The other car sped up, too. Dane executed a few turns for the benefit of the opposition, who turned with him. An office park lay ahead. Dane turned into the empty parking lot and raced across the blacktop until a curb blocked further progress. On the other side of the curb was a patch of grass and some trees and no lights. He bolted from the car and ran into the darkness with gun in hand. For a moment the other car spotlighted him. A burst of automatic fire said the ungodly did not want him running into the dark, but Dane kept running until he found a large tree beside which he could drop flat.

One man climbed out of the car and advanced into the dark. The driver backed up and went around the other side of the property. Blocking escape. Fine with Dane. Easier to deal with one thug than two. The silhouette coming his way soon blended with the darkness. Dane breathed slowly and lay still. One hand covered his stainless automatic so no hint of light would reflect and give away his position. The grass was wet from a fresh watering and the water soaked through Dane's clothes, but in spite of that he began to fall in love with his hiding spot. There he was comfortable and concealed and the tree's trunk was thick enough to stop the projectile from a howitzer. Or so he told himself as his pulse raced. To survive combat, one had to believe he was invincible; perhaps the other chap believed it, too. He had to fight the doubt that intruded, push the thought out of his mind, because he knew he wasn't.

The other man stopped and dropped into a squat, then stretched out. He started moving forward a few inches at a time.

Dane lost sight of the man's profile for a moment. He looked off to one side, letting his peripheral vision take over. There. Something moved. Dane turned back and saw a bit of light wink off the other man's wristwatch. Only a few feet separated Dane from the gunman, but the gunman's course was taking him away from Dane in a diagonal direction.

The wristwatch flashed again.

The ghosts of battles past were telling Dane to take the option. Now.

Dane fired twice. The orange flash from the muzzle ruined his night vision and he could no longer see much of anything, but that didn't stop him from rising and rushing toward the gunman's position.

Dane almost tripped on the man's legs.

The man lay still, his side torn open from the pair of fat .45 hollow points. Dane rolled the man onto his back. He was quite dead. A nice bit of shooting, that was. Dane put away the .45 and rolled the man back onto his stomach. He wore a long black coat. Dane removed the coat and put it on. The sleeves hung past his wrists. No matter. He tied it around his waist, picked up the dead man's submachine gun, and hoofed it back to his car.

He called Nina and quickly told her where to find the car and to get her booty over to the business park to pick it up. She responded carefully but still slurred some of the words.

"I can't see remember, darling? My booty will remain in this tub for as long as it wants and since it is attached to the rest of me that means I am not going anywhere but thank you for the call and please don't get killed because I look absolutely horrible in black."

Dane threw the phone into the car. She was no good to

him. He'd have to call Russo to collect the car. It had to be out of there before the cops showed up.

He scanned the car for the gunman's vehicle. And there it was, rolling back this way. Time to take advantage of the blood spatter on the coat.

Dane lurched toward the other car, pressing his left arm against his middle and covering part of his face with his other hand. The gunman's car stopped. The driver hollered something in another language; Dane responded with a loud groan. He pulled at the back door, but it was locked. The driver hit the lock and Dane crawled onto the backseat. He moaned again. The driver said something that sounded reassuring and twisted the car around in a tight U-turn and sped off into the street.

Presently the car stopped, and the driver shut off the engine. Dane peeked long enough to see that they were parked outside. He could not see the area around them. The driver climbed out of the car, opened the back door, and Dane shot him in the face.

Dane hopped out of the car. His move had not been tactically sound, but it had been the only thing to do. As soon as the driver had a look at him, all bets were off. Dane advanced on the small bungalow. They were in the countryside just beyond Mestre city limits, with a highway a few hundred yards away. A few cars traveled along it, and Dane knew from studying a map of the region earlier that the road would take him back to town. But first things first.

The bungalow's front door had not opened. Why had nobody responded to the pistol shot? Dane tried the knob. Locked. A blast from the .45 broke the lock and he went inside. He kept close to the entryway wall, listening. Lights burned in the room beyond but there were no voices, not even a television. Dane stepped into the kitchen/living room, but not a soul met him there. Down a hallway, there were three bedrooms. The first two each had twin bunks. Male clothing items in each room. Dane opened the third door. A lone mattress sat in a corner, an unconscious man lay on the floor, and a woman's pink sweater lay on the carpet.

Dane examined the man. A big lump was growing out of the top of the man's head.

He picked up the sweater. It bore the scent of some brand of perfume, something a young woman might choose. He'd seen the sweater before.

Leila Russo had been wearing it.

But where was she?

Dane put away the gun and went back outside. Footsteps shuffled behind him. He whirled around, going for his gun, but the two men who climbed out of the bushes were on top of him before he could make another move. One of them jammed a stun gun into his neck. The stun gun went *snap crackle* and the lights went out before he heard *pop*.

Chapter Six

When Leila Russo saw the man in the black car at the hotel, she thought it was her father. He had sent the note, after all, and while that type of communication was irregular, there was no reason to doubt the source. But as she bent to get into the car, she saw the man's face. It was not her father. He held a gun. She screamed and started to run, but a second man leapt out the other side and shoved her in. Her head slammed into the doorframe. As the door was slammed shut behind her, she clawed at the first man's face and batted his gun away as he tried to smack her with it. She shoved it away the first time, but not the second, and the man smacked her. She slumped against the seat and was conscious of the car's speeding away after another moment, but that was all.

She woke up and retched a little. She had been dropped onto a bare mattress in an otherwise empty room. Bars covered the window. She examined her clothes. They were rumpled but intact. She had not been molested. She stood up but had to balance against the wall for a moment. She loosened her heels and kicked them away. She tried the door, but it was locked. She slammed her palms against the door and shouted, "Let me out of here!" She pounded some more and eventually the door opened. She stepped back.

A dark-skinned young man held a small submachine gun, and he pointed it at her.

"You will be quiet," he said. "We will not hurt you. You want to go home, you will behave."

"You're a jerk."

The man lowered the gun. Leila watched his arms to see if his muscles tensed prior to striking her. Her last boyfriend had hit her once, only once, and she'd known the blow was coming because he'd flexed his arm before he swung. This man did not do that. He pulled the door shut and left her there alone.

Leila Russo put her hands on her hips and stared at the closed door.

She looked at her leather belt, thinking it could be a weapon, but it was too thick. They'd left her stilettos, though. Those could be very nice weapons. She smiled as she hefted one of the pumps and felt the tip of the six-inch heel. These goons weren't very smart. Her father had taught her long ago that fashion accessories such as heels and long, sharp earrings could be effective weapons if somebody attacked her.

She pitied other girls who didn't have a Papa like the one she had.

Leila put the heel down and sat on the mattress. She didn't know how many men were guarding her, but that wouldn't be the case for long.

The sky darkened through the barred window, and when her tummy growled, she wondered when they'd bring dinner. Presently the door opened and another man, this one younger than the first, with a wiry frame and thick black hair, entered with a food tray. His weapon was slung over his shoulder. He made eye contact with her but said nothing.

She stood up as he put the tray on the carpet.

"You're cute," she said.

He smiled.

"Thanks for the grub." She made a show of pulling off her sweater. The camisole underneath gave him the peek she wanted. She dropped the sweater on the mattress. "Anything else?"

The man's eyes were back on hers. He shook his head and pulled the door shut.

Leila smiled and ate the food. They had provided a spork as the only utensil. They were idiots. No silverware but they left her shoes?

Several hours ticked by. She heard men talking and pressed her ear to the crack between the door and the door-frame. Somebody was departing—two men? They asked another if he was sure he could take care of "the woman" alone. He assured them he could. The wiry kid? The front door shut. She paced back and forth while she formulated a plan. She couldn't stay cooped up waiting for Papa when the goons might get impatient and send him one of her fingers. Or worse.

She grabbed one of the pumps and pounded on the door. "Hey! Buttface! Open up!"

A few minutes of pounding later, the door opened. She stepped back. Both hands were behind her back and the pump was gripped in her right. She squeezed her arms so her breasts peeked up a little, and when the wiry kid stuck his head in, that's the first thing he saw.

"What?"

"I need to pee, dummy."

"Hold it till morning."

"Are you nuts?" Two steps forward. "Do you want me to make a mess on the floor?"

"Hold it."

"Bring me a bucket at least."

"You will—"

She swung as hard as she could and felt the tip of the heel dig into his temple. He let out a cry, stumbling forward; she followed up with another bash, and another, as he tumbled onto the carpet. He was breathing but he wasn't moving. Leila stepped into the heel and hopped over to the other, stepping into that, and then she locked the door behind her and ran down the hall.

Leila Russo walked along the shoulder of the road for just over an hour before she flagged down a car. An older couple. She gave them a story about having a fight with her boyfriend and him leaving her on the roadside, and the couple gave her a lift back into town. They dropped her off at the hotel, per her instructions, and she raced into the lobby and collected her key from the desk clerk.

Up in her room she collapsed on the bed. Her body shook. Two mini bottles of vodka and a shower and a change of clothes calmed her down. She called Papa. Her father let out a shout of joy when he heard her voice, but as she told the story he shushed her. He said he would send somebody over right away to collect her and she could tell her story in person.

Chapter Seven

Steve Dane awoke on a couch.

A man stepped into view. "Hello, Steve."

Dane groaned. "Len. Hey. Wow. Did a truck hit me?"

Len Lukavina had thick dark hair and dark eyes. One side of his face appeared warped, and the corner of one eye drooped and the lid didn't move when he blinked.

Lukavina was the man Dane had rescued from the burning helicopter, but not fast enough. Lukavina had taken the most punishing blast of the explosion, nearly burning to death. So extensive had been the damage that no amount of plastic surgery could fully erase the effects. Lukavina had never been an undercover man, and with such a distinctive appearance he never could be, but he still made it into the field, working with a team of agents who did the heavy lifting while he remained behind the scenes.

Once they had served together in the Marines and then the CIA. Now Dane worked for himself, while Lukavina remained a faithful Company man.

"What are you doing here?" Lukavina said.

Dane put a hand to his head. Why did Tasers cause so

much pain throughout the whole body?

"Here?" Dane said. "Somebody *brought* me here. I didn't set out to visit this place."

"I mean what are you—you *know* what I mean."

"Do you expect me to talk?"

"No, Steve, I expect you to stay out of our way."

Dane slowly sat up. "We can help each other. Tell me what you're doing."

"Ha."

"Then I'll just sit and stare at you."

Lukavina pressed his lips together. "If you can behave," he said, "we'll talk."

"Where am I?"

"Safe house."

"Did your people see the girl leave before I got there?"

"What girl?"

"I thought so. Day late and a dollar short."

In the kitchen Lukavina poured each of them a glass of Perrier. Dane leaned against the counter but managed to stay on his feet.

"Uncle Sam doesn't allow us to drink in the field any-more," Lukavina said.

"Anymore? I don't recall that he ever did. But when did that stop you?"

"The day a couple of prissy knuckleheads were assigned to my team who tell the boss everything that's not proper. You can't trust anybody *under* 30 these days."

"Cheers," Dane said, "to the new generation of self-ap-pointed do-gooders. May they join all the dead lawyers at the bottom of the ocean."

They sat at the kitchen table.

"Now," the CIA man said, "talk."

"You first. Tell me the score. Why is the Agency interested in Milani?"

"Why are you?"

"Okay, fine." Dane sipped the Perrier. The bubbles burned going down his throat. It wasn't his favorite drink. Always gave him hiccups. He gave the other man a rundown of his adventures in Mestre so far. The CIA man didn't drink any water but instead made circles with the cup until Dane finished.

"We're on two separate threads of the same case," Lukavina said.

"What does that mean?"

"Milani has a backpack nuke. He wants to sell it to al-Qaeda."

"And I may botch the sting."

"Yup."

This was not what Dane had expected to learn. He kept his cool and drank some more Perrier. "You gonna drink yours?"

"No," Lukavina said. "This crap makes me hiccup. But I don't understand how Milani expects to deal with the terrorists and Russo and not somehow get burned."

"Revenge knows no patience," Dane said. "Plus, he doesn't want payment for the girl's return. He has no intention of returning her. He wants to kill her and make her father suffer. He's going to strike while he has the chance. He may not get another one."

"But you said she was gone when you raided the house."

"Uh-huh. Looks like she escaped. Smart girl. But she's on the run somewhere and I need to find her."

"Uh-huh."

"Tell me more about this nuke. There is only one type that I can think of that matches your description," Dane said. "The SADM."

"Correct."

The Special Atomic Demolition Munitions unit had been a product of the Cold War. Cylindrical in shape, with no exterior markings, it weighed only 50 pounds. The plan, on paper, for the deployment of such a weapon had been for a pair of special operations personnel to parachute behind the Iron Curtain and plant the bomb in specified locations of strategic importance. In the event of war, the SADMs would be set off. They were never deployed but had remained in the US inventory for decades until the signing of a classified disarmament treaty that eliminated such weapons on both sides.

"How did an old Mafia man get his hands on a SADM? They've all been dismantled by now. Did somebody make him one?"

"No. He found one buried in the ground."

"Explain *that* to me. What happened to the teams that work specifically to make sure no loose nukes end up on the market?"

The Agency had not only teams looking for wayward nuclear weapons, but other units that ran sting operations against potential purchasers. These agents would advertise their desire to sell a nuke and attract clients, and those clients would be busted and interrogated for more information. The sting units operated on the theory that if terrorists had no idea whether or not a nuke sale was a trap, they would stop trying to buy them.

At least until a rogue country built them one.

"In 1989 there was a special ops general named Wolski," Lukavina said. "He had a stellar career and was able to finagle an assignment to special ops and was in charge of the SADM inventory. Huge anti-communist. Members of his family had fought the commies all the way back before World War I, and many of those family members were killed, either in battle or executed after. When the Berlin Wall fell and the Soviets gave up, he wasn't happy. He wanted one final battle to wipe them off the face of the earth.

"What he did was get two of his best guys to parachute into Russia with a pair of SADMs. Somebody close to him turned him in, and we rounded up the three of them. We agreed to reduce the charge against him if he told us where the nukes were buried, but he only gave up one until we put the offer in writing. We found that one without trouble, but then Wolski and his men tried to escape and were killed. We never located the second nuke. Since they were set to detonate by remote control, we had plenty of time, but somebody else got there first."

"One of our people? Dug it up and sold it?"

"Exactly. Wolski had one other person working for him that managed to elude us when the others were arrested. She stayed under the radar for the longest time but then decided to move the other nuke. We have her in custody already. That's why we know who has the weapon."

"So why not pounce on Milani right now?"

"We want the tangos, too."

"Of course, you do."

"Obtaining a nuke is top priority with al-Qaeda. We've intercepted enough coded messages to confirm that. We need the buyers to lead us to their bosses so we can round up the lot of them, not just onesies and twosies."

"How did Milani get the nuke? Is he the middleman for somebody?"

"Yes," the CIA agent said. "There's a new arms dealer on the scene. All we know about her is her codename. The Duchess."

"And how did you learn about her?"

"Old-fashioned grunt work."

"Nuts. You have somebody on the inside."

Lukavina smiled. "I hope your stunt won't scare Milani off."

"He won't go anywhere," Dane said, "while Russo and his daughter are still alive."

Chapter Eight

Dane returned to the hotel and found Nina once again sawing logs. He sat on the edge of the bed a moment. The after-effects of the Taser strike had faded, and he felt normal again. What he needed now was rest. He called Russo to make a report, but before he could say anything about his discovery, Russo told him Leila had escaped on her own. Dane felt a weight leave his shoulders. He arranged to meet Russo once the sun came up.

Nina continued snoring. At least the accordion player had taken the night off. Dane undressed and went out like a light once he crawled under the covers.

In the late afternoon, with Nina complaining that the vintner gods were playing bongos in her head, Dane visited Dominico Russo as arranged. He settled on the couch. Russo smiled as another person entered the room.

"Mr. Dane, meet my daughter, Leila."

Steve Dane jumped to his feet. "Hello," he said.

The woman's mouth remained a flat line as she looked Dane up and down. The mod outfit he had seen her in previously was gone, replaced by simple blue jeans and white T-shirt. Her black hair was tied back, but a few loose strands dangled near her ears.

"Is this the man you hired, Papa?"

"He is."

"Thank you, Mr. Dane, but I didn't need your help."

"You got lucky."

"I should have waited for you to come storming in with your horse and lance?"

"Leila, that's enough," her father said.

Leila dropped onto the other end of the couch. Dane resumed his seat. Russo motored near Dane.

"My apologies," Russo said.

Leila, still not smiling, stared at a spot on the carpet.

To Dane he said, "I shall honor our arrangement. You will be paid for—"

"No. I didn't finish the job."

"Mr. Dane—"

"I work for my money, Nico," Dane said. "And there is another way I can earn it, if you want to put Milani in a box for keeps."

"Explain."

Dane told him the situation with Milani's al-Qaeda meeting. Russo's cheeks flared.

"He's doing that?"

"Apparently he's an agent for a new arms dealer calling herself the Duchess. Does that name mean anything to you?"

"I have not heard of her."

Leila jumped in. "Where's Milani if he wasn't at the place I was held at?"

"He won't be far away," Dane said. "Nico, did he have a preferred hideout when you two were running the show?"

"Expensive hotels and public places. Usually travelled with two or three bodyguards."

"How about this," the girl said. "They're probably out looking for me. Why don't I wander around and get caught again? I can tell you where he's at."

"No," Russo said.

"That won't work," Dane said. "You'll be taken to another hideout nowhere near Milani."

"This is my fight, too."

"You will stay here, Leila."

The woman huffed and stormed out.

Russo smiled a little. "She is much like her mother."

"Your wife must have been some lady."

"She was." Russo eyes drifted elsewhere, and he remained silent.

"Leila is very sharp. She is not like other girls her age. Perhaps she also takes after her father?"

Russo only nodded.

The door swung open and Junior came in, breathless. "Leila took one of my guns! She's gone!"

Russo issued orders for Junior and Pops to go after her and to grab the other staff members if they were needed.

Dane and Russo sat in silence for a few minutes after Junior departed and did not talk any further. Dane excused himself and returned to the hotel. He had his own ideas on how to track Leila down, but he needed Nina's help. He figured Leila was right about Milani's men still looking for her. And if that were truly the case, one of those men, with appropriate pressure, would tell Dane where Milani was hiding.

The little hothead, he thought, might prove useful after all.

The gun kept digging into Leila Russo's belly, and she didn't think the jacket she had grabbed prior to her exit hid the bulge. Hiding guns wasn't her thing. It wasn't at all like she saw in the movies. Everybody's eyes seemed to be on her, and she knew any second a cop would spot her and arrest her, but she had to keep moving, stay visible in obvious places and attract the attention she was sure was out there.

She window-shopped, using that as an excuse to look around a lot, yet nobody noticed.

She ordered coffee at three different cafes, and sat outside, and nobody watched her. A little while later, she required a bathroom visit and stood in the stall a few extra moments, despite the urgency, trying to figure out where to put the gun. She stuck it on the coat hook, where it dangled, and she stared at it so she wouldn't forget it was there, and, alone, tried a few poses in the mirror to reassure that the gun did not show.

Leila Russo continued wandering the streets yet attracted no more attention than the roving eyes of males. She was not unaware of her attractiveness, and such peeks were normal. And this was one time when that type of attention wasn't what she craved.

Where were the creeps?

How hard was it to get kidnapped again?

Her father and his bodyguards would be out looking for her too. And Papa would be pissed. But she had to do this. If he was going to ask others to risk their lives for her, she had to do something to contribute to the effort so those people could do what Papa had hired them to do. There was no sign of Luigi or Pasquale either.

Then her stomach rumbled. She found a McDonald's and sat in the back corner with her Chicken McNuggets, and halfway through the meal a man in a tan suit entered and scanned the dining area. His eyes landed on hers, and not because he was another dude who thought she was cute. There was something more behind his eyes—something that made her shiver. He ordered at the counter and sat down at the opposite end of the restaurant, but Leila saw him peek at her enough to know that she had finally picked up one of the goons looking for her.

The man had close-cropped hair. He filled the suit too well and glanced at her the wrong way before dialing a cell phone. She finished her meal. On the street, she spotted Hunky Dude keeping a discreet distance, but he stayed with her even as she jogged through a crosswalk and walked two more blocks away from the restaurant. Stopping to check out more window displays, she stole another glance back, and her shadow was on the phone again.

Finally!

She kept going, passing a line of shops, crossing in front of an alley—

The hand that covered her mouth blocked her scream, and there was no way to fight the strength in the arms that pulled her from the sidewalk. Breath left her as she was forced against the alley wall. The hand moved away. Leila breathed hard and fast as she stared into the face of Steve Dane.

"You might as well have had a flashing sign on your head," he told her.

"You—"

He shushed her and snatched her gun, and when Hunky Dude came abreast of the alley, Dane swung the gun and conked the interloper over the head. Just then Nina screeched up in the car and Dane loaded the man into the back seat. Leila watched from the alley. Dane came back, grabbed her, and shoved her into the front seat next to Nina.

Chapter Nine

"What if somebody saw us?" Leila said.

"So what?" Dane said. "Never let witnesses get in your way."

Leila let out a string of curses as she sank down in the passenger seat.

"You're sharp, Leila, but leave this to the professionals," Dane said.

Nina patted the young woman's leg. "His definition of professional is different than mine, honey."

"You two are insane."

"Only a little."

Nina steered the car onto a highway. Dane slapped their captive. The other man moaned, waking with a start. Dane slammed him back against the seat. "Behave yourself. We're going to have a little chat."

"Why should I tell you anything?"

"I'll let you go. Live to fight another day."

"How do I know I can trust you?"

"You can't."

Hunky Dude, still breathing hard, didn't blink for a

moment. When he did, Dane knew he had the man right where he wanted him.

"Where's your boss hiding?"

"Milani's hiding at a farm," the other man said. "Off the N5."

"There are a lot of farms off the N5."

"His has a single-story house. No animals. It's the only one with no animals. That's all I know!"

"Hardly." Dane pressed the .45 into the man's gut. "There's more." He jabbed once with the barrel. The prisoner winced.

"Okay, okay!"

"Talk."

"He visits the Testaccio Club every night. He likes the singer there. Table near the stage."

Dane scooted back and put away his gun. The prisoner relaxed a little, moved his foot an inch, and Dane whipped out the gun again. "I told you to behave."

"We made a deal."

"We did. Pull over, darling."

Nina slowed the car and pulled off the shoulder. They were still within city limits, but it would be a long walk to wherever the turncoat intended to go. Nina turned around and leveled her own gun at the prisoner while Dane returned his gun to its holster and took out a wallet. He handed the man a wad of bills.

"Get out."

Hunky Dude stared at the money. "You're going to shoot me in the back."

"I won't. She might."

Nina smiled. "I haven't shot anybody in weeks. Going through withdrawal."

"Get out now," Dane said.

The prisoner bolted, clawing at the door handle, launching onto the roadway, the door still open. He ran clear across the road. Dane pulled the door shut and sat back. Nina started driving again.

Leila said, "Was that smart?"

"You saw him crack," Dane said. "If he reports back, he'll have a hard time lying. Milani will know he talked. He has no choice but to run."

"Now what do we do?" Nina said.

"Let's check out that singer," Dane said.

The Testaccio Club wasn't the music-thumping dance club Dane had first thought of. It had the look of a comfortable tavern catering to middle-aged folks; judging by the clientele at the tables and bars, they had succeeded in attracting exactly that. Dark colors, low lighting, muted voices; it wasn't a place the party scene would go. Dane, Nina and Leila found a booth and scooted in. A waiter appeared and took their orders for drinks, and Leila added an appetizer plate to the selection. The singer/piano combo on the small stage held the attention of the patrons. The singer, a blonde in a slinky black dress, sung in a low voice but exercised great range when the tune called for it.

Leila scanned the faces of those sitting near the stage.

"He won't be in the open," Dane said.

"What do you mean?"

"Look along the wall. Milano will keep his back to it. Same as us."

"Guess I didn't notice."

The drinks arrived. Leila picked at the appetizer with a fork. She didn't offer Dane and Nina any, but that didn't stop Nina from spearing a portion. Dane ignored the food. His mind was focused on their surroundings, on the mission. The four tables along the wall were full, and he spotted Milani almost right away, or at least the best suspect. The man sat in the booth with a woman on one side and two heavies on either end. He had no hair and a crooked nose and was pushing 70. He drank a double scotch, no ice. The woman sipped a martini. The heavies watched everybody but the stage.

"See him?" Nina said.

"I think that's him."

Nina swallowed some of her drink. "I hope you aren't going to do anything stupid, like going over to talk to him."

"No. I have another idea."

"Are we leaving?" Leila said, holding a piece of cheese.

"Finish your snack," Dane said.

After delivering Leila back to her father, Dane and Nina returned to their hotel suite. Dane went out on the deck, lit a Glandon and selected a number on his cell phone. Nina joined him, holding a glass of wine. Dane listened to the line ring a few times.

"Yes?" the voice on the other end said.

"It's me."

"Hey, ugly," Devlin Stone said.

Stone had worked with Dane in the 30-30 Battalion, and they still aided each other in various buccaneering activities. Stone worked a smuggling operation in Europe, running guns, cigarettes, liquor, and pistachio nuts. He had a dedicated crew of misfits, two homes and a string of legitimate front companies that provided the necessary paper trail for his earnings.

"I'm in Italy. Have you heard of a new arms broker called the Duchess?"

"Only rumors."

"Like what?"

"She's currently unloading a dozen crates of US weapons."

"Interesting."

"You working?"

"Yes," and Dane told him the story.

"Sounds fun," Stone said. "What do you need from me?"

"I'd like to build a phony backpack nuke, and I thought you'd be the best man for the job."

"I can't believe what you're thinking."

"I'm thinking it," Dane said, "and together you and I can pull it off."

"We'll get killed trying."

"When has that ever stopped us?"

"True. When do you want this shoddy bomb case full of used pinball machine parts?"

"Is now too soon?"

"See you in a few hours."

Dane hung up. He turned to Nina.

"Here comes the cavalry," she said.

Chapter Ten

Dane and Nina had time for lunch before picking up Stone, so they
ate sandwiches at a street café. They both enjoyed what
the proprietor called a Godmother Sandwich. The French
bread was well toasted and crispy and didn't get soggy.
Several layers of Italian ham and salami and prosciutto and
cheese and jalapeño with vinaigrette made up the ensemble, and they almost forgot about the two men who were
spying on them from a car across the street.

"Cops or bad guys?" Nina said.

He looked over her shoulder. "Cops."

Detective Lazzaro Palermo strolled up the sidewalk,
grabbed an empty chair, and pulled it over to Dane's
table. He sat.

"I'm getting in the habit of interrupting your meals,"
the detective said.

"That's okay. Want a sandwich?"

As Palermo started to answer, the car with the two
spies drove off.

"Were those your men?"

"Yes. I actually have work to do in this city and do not

have the time to be chasing rabbits named Steve Dane, so I had two of my junior detectives keep an eye on you until I could break away to have this conversation."

"I'm all ears."

"You're causing trouble," the detective said.

"I am not," Dane said. "I am contributing to the economy of Italy and enjoying the sights of this town."

"You are causing trouble," the detective repeated. "Otherwise I would not have the US State Department or Interpol asking me to bring you in for questioning."

"Forget it. They have their own people."

"They do not want to step on our toes, Mr. Dane. Apparently, you have no such inhibitions."

Dane swallowed a bite of sandwich.

"So far," Palermo said, "I cannot say for sure that you have committed crimes in my city, though I have one or two ideas. It would be very smart if you left the country and did not return for some time. I will even suggest that you never come back."

"That oversteps your boundaries a little, Detective."

The detective shrugged. "You have been warned." Palermo stood up and walked away.

Dane wiped his mouth and drank some water.

"Your CIA friend talked," Nina said.

"He had to report. He has a few people on his team that like to tattletale."

"You can't trust anybody these days."

"I can trust you," he said.

"Only until you stop putting out," she said.

"Look who's talking." He checked his watch. "Finish up. Stone's plane lands soon."

Devlin Stone entered the terminal at Marco Polo Airport in a pressed blue suit that clashed with his shaggy hair. He always wore the mop a little long and some of it rested atop his ears. He was constantly brushing the hair away because it irritated him but refused to cut the source of the problem.

Stone had already cleared customs and carried only suitcases. Dane wondered where the rest of his equipment was. Stone only smiled. He did not want to risk bringing the phony bomb case and assorted small bits on the plane, so he had some of his men bring it into the country by their usual nefarious means. The equipment would be waiting at a drop. Within an hour they had retrieved the gear and then took the large steamer trunk back to the hotel suite.

The trunk held the cylindrical container that could pass as a SADM, complete with an accurate backpack. The trunk contained Stone's personal weapons, Heckler & Koch submachine guns and ammunition for Dane and Nina, grenades, other explosive goodies and a Geiger counter.

Reconnaissance of Milani's farm was first on the list, and the trio drove out to the location provided by their informant. Nina, afraid the former prisoner had lied, doubted the farm would be there, but it was there, the one-story house surrounded by empty pens and open ground. The four SUVs sitting out front indicated signs of life. A road wound past the house, and Dane, Nina and Stone watched from a rise overlooking the road and house. Every now and then a man would exit the house, wander around a bit and re-enter. He was not a ranch hand. His big coat could easily hide artillery. It looked like the right place.

To make sure, they went back to the Testaccio Club that

night to observe Milani again. There was no need to follow Milani's vehicle back to the farm, because at the end of the night he climbed into one of the SUVs they had seen in front of the house.

Dane said, "We have enough open area for a nice gun battle should the need arise. Our major obstacle is the CIA team."

"Where do you think they're hiding?" Nina said. "And did they see us stomping through the bush today?"

"We'd know if they did," Dane said.

Stone said, "I spotted a shack on one side of the house that I think leads to a basement. The SADM is probably hidden down there. If we can get around the guards and not cause too much of a fuss—"

"Big if," Dane said, "but I don't know of any other way."

"Helicopter," Nina said. "Do you think Russo has one?"

"I know he does," Dane said. "That will be our extraction. We'll go in by car first. The Agency people won't notice another car on the highway. Once the action starts, driving away will be out of the question, but we can fly."

"I guess you were right about having friends in low places," Nina said.

"I'm always right, baby, but you won't admit it."

Stone said, "Let's get this phony bomb assembled. I'm not carrying it."

"Nor am I," Nina said.

"I'll carry the bomb," Dane said. "Good grief, do I have to do all the work around here?"

Stone displayed the HK submachine guns he had brought with flour- ish. The Heckler & Koch UMP, the variant chambered for the .45 ACP, had earned the same reputation for reliability and ease of operation as the legendary HK MP5.

"I installed a forward handgrip," Stone explained, "because it will help you control full-auto fire." Stone added that the HK was easy to carry because the shoulder stock folded closed.

But Dane decided he couldn't carry the HK and the SADMs, so he had to pass on the weapon; Nina didn't mind. "I get your ammo," she said.

A short chat with Dominico Russo secured the "retired" capo's helicopter. Pops and Junior would fly the chopper. Dane didn't like that idea but there was no other choice. As long as the pair showed up on time, he wouldn't complain.

The hardest part of the plan was getting into the house. Dane hoped that the shack Stone had seen indeed led to the basement. If it didn't, and he needed to search a little, Stone and Nina planned to keep the troops engaged long enough to give Dane the time he needed to find the real SADM and replace it with the fake, thereby setting up Milani to be murdered by his al-Qaeda contacts once they realized he had cheated them. Russo's vendetta would be over, and Lukavina could follow the terrorists back to home base.

Thinking about it as evening neared, Dane decided that it wasn't the best operation he had ever planned; hopefully it wouldn't also be the worst.

Chapter Eleven

Dane waited in front of the fence closest to the side of the farmhouse. His unobstructed view included the door of the side shack. The night was cold and quiet so far. He didn't want to move until Nina and Stone started shooting. Any second now…

He jumped at the first chatter of gunfire. In the house, lights went off. A pair of troopers launched from the back door and worked their way around. Dane wanted to take a pot shot with his .45 but the distance didn't favor the effort. He let them go by. More automatic weapons fire. The flash and flame of a grenade. Screams. Dane waited while the pair cleared the front. With the phony SADM secured over his shoulders and the Detonics Scoremaster in his right fist, Dane vaulted over the fence and landed hard on the ground opposite. The 50 pounds' worth of phony SADM made his sprint feel like a long plod, but the hard dirt beneath his boots at least provided necessary traction. The standard weight of the rucksack he'd used in the Marines had been 30 to 120 pounds, which made the faux SADM light by comparison, but it still required effort. The gunfire and explosions continued, though at a sporadic rate now; he had no way of knowing which side was winning. Everyone on his side had a wireless radio, but they were maintaining total silence until Dane had achieved his objective.

Dane reached the doorway. A tug on the handle. Locked. Dane shot off the lock. He descended concrete steps into the darkened basement, lighting the way with a pen flash. The needle on the Geiger counter, strapped to his left wrist, jittered. Stone's guess had been right on the mark. The real SADM was indeed somewhere in the basement.

Gunfire and explosions continued above. Nina and Stone were giving the troops a real run for the money. Dane reached the concrete bottom and shined his flash around. The basement contained the usual accumulation of junk, some of it with such a layer of dust that it must have been abandoned by the home's previous occupant. Dane wandered over to a long chest, and the Geiger's needle jumped. Bingo.

Two blows with the butt of the Scoremaster broke the lock, and Dane lifted the lid. In the case, nestled on its back, lay the real SADM, the olive-drab backpack about as bland and unassuming as anything.

Dane lowered his own pack and holstered the .45.

Light appeared at the top of the opposite stairway as the inside door opened. Dane ducked behind a stack of boxes. Two men stood in the doorway a moment, then began their descent, pulling the door shut. One used a flashlight to navigate downward. Neither spoke but Dane heard their heavy breathing. Milani wanted the SADM checked. No surprise there. With their sweaty faces and labored breathing, they must have come from defending the front. Did their removal from that part of the action mean Nina and Stone had been killed or captured? Dane took out the Detonics .45 and quietly clicked off the safety. The first man reached the ground and shined the light at the open SADM. He swung the light to his partner and started to say something. The second man, now spotlighted, made for the perfect target. Dane fired twice. The man fell back without a cry, but his head cracked loud on the concrete. As the first man turned, Dane fired again and again. The flashlight clattered on the ground before its owner landed. Dane went to the body and pulled it away from the SADM. He put the pistol away and started to grab the real nuclear device. The upper door opened again. A man called down to his compatriots. Dane grabbed the flashlight carrier's submachine gun and hosed the doorway. The man in the doorway jerked with random hits and fell back. Dane plucked a grenade from his combat vest and tossed the orb upward; the explosion kicked the door off the frame and set the hallway wall on fire. As the flames spread to the doorway, Dane slung the real SADM over his left shoulder and the phony over his right. There was no more time for games. He had to try to make it out with both and maybe lose the "real" one along the way. Keying his radio as he ascended to the top, he said, "Got it, let's go."

Silence in his ear.

Dane kept climbing. He keyed the radio again. "Dev? Nina?"

"Here," came Nina's reply. "A little occupied."

"Break contact," he said. Dane reached the ground level and started running for the fence. The heavy weight of each pack really slowed him this time. His lungs burned and his legs flared with strain as he tried to keep up at least a jogging speed. Bright lights hit him. An engine grumbled. Dane stopped as one of the SUVs plowed through the dirt in front of him, stopped, and the doors swung open. Gunmen piled out. Dane let the SADMs fall from his back and snapped out his pistol. He squeezed each trigger repeatedly. The two who climbed out the driver's side went down. The other two, hunkered at either end of the vehicle, had some semblance of cover. Dane shot the gunman at the front of the SUV in the head. The last, who had only enough time to dig out his machine pistol, fell to the final round from the Scoremaster.

No time to reload. Dane put the gun away, grabbed the packs by their straps and dragged them along the dirt as he continued his trot for the fence.

Stone's voice in his ear. "Coming up at seven o'clock."

Dane didn't turn. He knew Stone and Nina would be behind him. He stopped at the fence, dropped to one knee and reloaded the Detonics. The two figures running his way, each cradling a submachine gun, did not match the other gunmen. Dane scanned the battleground. Smoke poured from the basement. Something burned at the front of the house as well. The smoke from each fire curled into the night sky. Stone and Nina reached him. He told Stone to grab one of the packs. Stone slung his HK and then the SADM pack and climbed over the fence. Dane did likewise. Nina hopped over last. The trio started running again.

Shortly the ground sloped uphill and Dane strained to keep going. Another engine whined. Dane turned at the sound of a crash. An SUV had plowed through the fence and was heading their way, bouncing up the incline. The vehicle stopped. The doors swung open.

"Keep going!" Nina shouted as she filled the vehicle with HK automatic fire. One gunman fell but the other scrambled back into the SUV. Nina reloaded on the run as the troopers emerged from the other side, their own automatic fire strafing the dirt. Nina triggered another long blast. Dane shouted to Stone, "Run!" and stopped, dropping his pack. He took out the Detonics, shouted for Nina to get clear and fired single shots at their pursuers. Nina raced past him. She called out to him, and he grabbed the pack and ran by her as she emptied another magazine. Once again, she reloaded as she ran, and Dane opened fire to cover her, but his single shots weren't connecting with the trio of troopers still running their way.

Dane fired again and again and grabbed the pack. He took two steps and fell headlong into the dirt; the large rock he'd tripped over lay beside his left ankle. He heard Nina shouting at him. More automatic fire from her weapon. Dane rolled onto his back with his pistol in both hands. The three figures charging at him were mere shadows against the black of the night. Dane fired once, twice, a third time. One man fell. Dane fired again. The slide locked back over the now empty magazine, and as Dane pawed for another, the last two were on him, pounding at his body with the butts of their rifles.

Presently the beating stopped. Dane's body relaxed into submission.

He heard a chopper whipping overhead.

Chapter Twelve

Dane woke up tied to a chair. The ponytailed blonde man from the earlier meeting at the park sat before him, smoking a cigarette. A bowl of spent butts lay at his feet. He'd been there some time, waiting. Dane's fuzzy vision focused. He spoke, but his dry throat deadened his usual tone.

"You again."

The ponytailed man smiled. He wasn't wearing black this time, but faded jeans and a blue button-down shirt. Black socks, no shoes. "Yup," he said. "Call me Eric. You've caused a lot of trouble."

"Not nearly enough."

"Nice try with the nuke. It's back where it belongs. We're going to have to block off the section of the house you almost burned to a crisp, but we'll make out."

"Your friends are coming soon, aren't they?"

"Tomorrow. Well, a little over ten hours from now, anyway."

Dane breathed deeply, but his middle flared. Had the beating broken anything? Pain spots covered his entire body. He couldn't isolate any particular location.

He'd given Stone back the phony SADM. Terrific.

A door opened behind Dane and another man, breathing heavily, entered. The man joined ponytailed Eric and regarded Dane with disinterest. He sported a rumpled look. The pinky of his left hand was missing.

"Mr. Milani, I presume," Dane said. "I'd offer to shake hands but I'm a little tied up."

The man cracked a smile and bowed a little. "The notorious Steve Dane. I could have used a man like you. Too bad you wasted your time with Russo. His days ended along ago."

"Spare me," Dane said. "A smart man would have waited until after his deal before settling old scores."

"Time was of the essence," Milani said. "I am not one to waste an opportunity."

Eric blew out a stream of smoke. "Is killing him really a good idea?"

"What do you mean?" Milani said.

"Al-Qaeda might like a trophy. Dane's been around the block a few times. He wasn't always a second-story man. I know for a fact—"

"You know spit," Dane said.

"Dane's cancelled some tango tickets in his time," the blonde man finished. "Al-Qaeda might like to have a little fun with him."

Milani watched his number two smoke, then nodded. "We'll see."

Milani left the room. Eric smiled through another cloud of smoke.

"Don't say I'm not looking out for you, Dane."

"Remind me to return the favor someday."

"Sure. I've always wanted to see a ghost."

Dane fell asleep in the chair, his head sagging against his chest. His arms and legs had long ago gone numb. When he awoke, it was because somebody was dragging the chair backward. Out of the room, down a hallway. Into a living room. He was propped in front of a fireplace. Like a decoration. The man behind the chair, a trooper, took a seat. Milani and Eric and another trooper sat around a coffee table. Rifles rested against the chairs the troopers occupied; Milani sat unarmed; Eric wore an automatic on his belt. Empty coffee cups and the remains of munchies cluttered the table.

"Don't I get an espresso?" Dane said.

"I figured you for the coffee-and-rum type," Milani said.

"You've misjudged me."

Sunlight blasted through the curtained windows. How much longer? He listened for the sounds of an arriving vehicle but heard nothing.

"How much is al-Qaeda paying you? Is it worth the thousands who are going to die when they use that nuke?"

"I'll be nowhere near the blast," Milani said.

Dane stopped talking. He couldn't feel his arms or legs or any strain because of their positions. He'd have to be carried out, one way or another. Could Nina and Stone, with Russo's help, pull off a rescue? Or had Lukavina and his remaining agents somehow neutralized them? Dane glanced around at the living room. It looked like a home anywhere in the world—it could have been his. Before the fireplace behind him was a rack of pokers. Good weapons, those. If only his arms worked.

The ghosts of battles past whispered in his ear. All was not lost. There was always something to cling to. Something unexpected.

Lukavina had an inside man.

Dane let out a laugh.

"What's so funny?" Milani said.

Dane turned his head. "This isn't over yet, Animal."

An engine rumbled outside. Milani, Eric, and the troopers stood up. Milani issued orders, and the troopers went to get the SADM.

Milani went out and personally escorted the two al-Qaeda agents back inside. Tea with milk all around. The terrorists, in their khakis and silk shirts and coats that obviously hid hardware, jabbered eagerly about the deal. One held a large stainless-steel briefcase. Milani told them about Dane, presenting him like an inanimate object. He boasted of Dane's terrorist kills. Friends of the agents, perhaps. The men agreed an American prisoner was always a good thing, regardless of his background, and this American looked valuable indeed. Perhaps, in his head, there was something that would help them kill more Americans.

Steve Dane spat blood on the carpet.

The troopers brought back the SADM, carrying it between them. The terrorists stood up and began examining the packaging, then opened it and examined the cylinder itself. Dane caught only brief glimpses of the object as they oohed and aahed. It looked like the real thing, indeed.

Eric stood near Dane's chair. He wasn't smoking this time.

One of the terrorists took out a screwdriver and removed the SADM's side panel. He froze for a short moment, then began uttering a string of words to his compatriot. He removed the top of the weapon and looked within, the jumped back and glared at Milani.

"What's the problem?" the Animal wanted to know.

"It's a *fake*! "said one of the terrorists. "Do you think we wouldn't check it top to bottom? Do you think we're *fools*?"

The two terrorists hauled machine pistols from under their coats. The troopers raised their rifles. The room exploded in a fury of muzzle blasts. Eric shoved Dane, and the chair toppled to the floor. Eric's gun cracked twice. Both terrorists dropped from the head shots. They'd already riddled the troopers, who lay dead, their rifles askew. Only Milani remained, and he'd dived between the couch and coffee table.

"Nice shooting, Eric!" the Animal said. He stood and brushed off the front of his shirt. "My God. What a mess."

"Sure is," Eric said, and shot Milani between the eyes. The old man remained upright a moment, then fell sideways against the couch. He flopped off the couch and back onto the carpet.

Dane looked up at Eric. The ponytailed man returned the smoking automatic to its holster.

"I'm John Foley," the ponytailed man said. "Central Intelligence Agency." He lifted Dane's chair and began slicing the ropes. "Take it easy."

"Did you know it was the fake the whole time?" Dane said as his limbs began to tingle.

"Yup."

Chapter Thirteen

Two days later Steve Dane sat poolside soaking up the sun. He wore a long-sleeved shirt, buttoned only at the bottom, and shorts that ended just above his knees, effectively concealing his scars.

He looked up from his magazine as Len Lukavina stepped through the pool gate wearing shorts and a T-shirt, the warped skin on his body in full view. Dane smiled but did not get off the lounger. Lukavina dropped into a squat beside Dane.

"Feeling better?"

"All fingers and toes accounted for," Dane said.

"You look like hell. You're practically painted with bruises and welts. You really want to be outside?"

"Since when do I care what people think?"

"You're full of smoke, you know that? Tell Stone thank you for bringing the real SADM by the house."

"Sure. He's back home but he'll appreciate the sentiments."

"He appreciated what you paid him even more, I'm sure," Lukavina said. "Have you talked to Russo?"

"I will tonight. There is one last bit of information I'd like to supply him with. You know what I mean."

"Who ratted out his daughter, yeah. Johnny was in on that." Lukavina removed a sealed envelope from a pocket of his shorts and passed it to Dane. The envelope was very thin. Dane held it up to the sun to see a folded sheet of paper inside.

"A name?"

"One name. Russo can close the account entirely."

"Is it one of his bodyguards?"

"No. Somebody higher in the organization. The guy was using Mafia money to pay his gambling debts and used the money Milani paid him to replace the money he took."

"How much trouble are you in?"

"Too much to count," the CIA man said. "Plus, my operation is only half completed. I didn't get to follow the terrorists back home."

"Tell them it's what happens in the field."

"You also cost us a lot of money and man-hours."

"We say *people*-hours now, Len."

Lukavina glared.

"What else could I do, Len? The client comes first."

"There was a time when your country came first."

"It still does, in my own way."

Len opened his mouth to say more but stopped. Dane knew he was going to disagree and maybe he had a point. The US would always be home, but Dane couldn't go back. Not yet.

"What's next for you?" the CIA man said.

"I came out here for a vacation," Dane said. "So far it's been everything but. I'm going to relax for a while and"—Dane smiled over Lukavina's shoulder—"have a good time with my lady."

Len Lukavina stood up as Nina returned carrying two martinis. She handed both to Dane and resumed her position on the neighboring lounger.

"Stop staring, Len," Dane said. "You look like you've never seen a woman before."

Nina said, "He's never seen a woman in a bikini like this before."

"She's still torturing me," Dane said. "There's this guy who plays his accordion all night. She won't—you know—until I do something about that."

Dane handed her a martini.

Lukavina took a second envelope from another pocket. "If you change your mind, here's the next link in the chain."

Dane made no move to take the envelope.

"Milani's next move," the CIA man said, "was to take al-Qaeda's money to Istanbul and hand it over to a contact there. We've also picked up some chatter in Paris, a man named Daudet. He might also be involved."

"You learned about it," Dane said. "Your people can handle it."

"My people and I are going to be on the bench for a week after this mess. You owe me one."

Lukavina dropped the envelope on the ground beside the lounger and departed with a wave.

Dane swallowed some of his drink.

"We have to follow that lead," Nina said.

"Don't start with me, baby."

"If this Duchess can acquire nuclear weapons, she needs to be stopped."

Dane set his drink down, donned a pair of sunglasses and lay back. "Relax and drink your vitamins. Let's just catch rays for a while."

"And then I'm going to Paris *with* or *without* you.

"I'll take Istanbul."

"I knew you were going to say that."

"What gave it away?"

"You can never tell Len no."

"For a whole list of reasons," Dane admitted.

Their final meeting with Russo and his daughter, over dinner, con-cluded with the capo's handing Dane a very large tote bag full of cash.

"If there is anything you ever need," Russo said at the end, "do not hesitate to call me."

Upon their return to the hotel, they were greeted in the lobby by Detective Palermo. He stood in front of them with folded arms.

"Whatever you are doing," he said, "I assume it is over?"

"What gives you that idea?"

"The US government no longer has any concern for you. We've gone two days without anything blowing up or finding people shot dead in the street or anywhere else for that matter. Whatever happened—"

"I don't know a thing about it, Detective."

"When are you leaving my country?"

"Soon. A few days. Haven't seen Venice yet."

"Right *now* is not soon enough, Mr. Dane."

Much later, around 3:05 a.m., as Dane and Nina lay in bed, the accordion started up again. More revelry accompanied the noise.

Nina stirred and jabbed Dane in the arm until he opened his eyes and muttered, "What?"

She said, "Are you going to do something?" She wore ugly flannel pajamas and green face cream that made her look like a lizard.

"Honey, I *can't* shoot him."

"Do *something*."

"Sucker punch?"

"Acceptable."

Dane tossed the covers aside and rolled out of bed. He dressed and stepped into his shoes. "Get that crap off your face," he said, "and be naked when I come back."

"Yes, darling."

Dane left the room to "introduce" himself to the accordion player.

Part II:
The Moving Target

Chapter Fourteen

Sean McFadden sat with crossed legs, his dark hair slicked back, in front of a small restaurant sipping a warm mug of black currant tea with a touch of milk. Under the table sat a metal briefcase. It was supposed to be full of money.

Most passersby weren't wearing a jacket, but nobody seemed out of place if they did. The weather was cool enough that one could do as he pleased. McFadden wore a light windbreaker, zipped halfway up, to hide the silenced Walther PPQ 9mm autoloader under his right arm.

Mixed with the vehicle noises and the heavy footsteps on the cobbled pavement were shouts from street vendors. From food carts spaced out on either side of the street, meat and chicken sizzled and the scents of curry and garlic wafted his way. McFadden took it all in but was not able to enjoy it. Maybe another time. Today he was working. His blue eyes missed no detail as he scanned the pedestrians and traffic, but there was only one person he was looking for. Everybody else was cannon fodder.

A freelance assassin in high demand, McFadden had not always worked for himself, but the IRA was long gone, except for its weak political elements and clusters of "freedom fighters" who claimed to be carrying on the fight but were really nothing more than thugs blowing stuff up for no reason. When a soldier lost his country, there was nothing left to fight for but his own pocketbook. Someday he would return home to a country free of the British scourge; that day was not today.

The busy market square at the center of Istanbul with its old stone buildings and maze of back alleys, had been his choice for the meeting. Today's assignment wouldn't be hard. Meet a courier who had a briefcase full of money not unlike the one under the table. Trade cases. Kill the man. McFadden's case was empty and there would be no need to bring it back with him, but he would bring the full one back to the Duchess.

The courier broke from the flow across the street. He walked with a limp and hustled between stopped cars, stepping onto the sidewalk almost directly across from McFadden. The courier was a mouse. Thin, pasty skin, straight hair, and his clothes didn't seem to fit. He made brief eye contact with McFadden, stopped, produced cigarettes and matches, lit up and dropped the matchbook. He kept walking. A trouble signal. McFadden rubbed his forehead. So much for easy. He drank down his tea and went over to pick up the matchbook. The courier had scribbled a phone number on the flap.

McFadden pocketed the matchbook and picked up the briefcase and went the opposite way the courier had gone.

A few blocks from the café, McFadden went into an alley and called the number on his cell phone.

"You better have a good reason," the assassin said.

"Milani and the al-Qaeda agents are dead, and the US has the nuke. There was somebody—"

"Wait." McFadden killed the connection and dialed another number. A woman answered. He said, "Milani and his contacts are dead. We do not, I repeat do not, have the nuke."

"The courier?" The woman spoke with a soft voice void of panic or emotion.

"Still alive."

"Complete the mission," she said. "I don't want any comebacks. And then I need you in Paris to deal with Daudet. He is a much more pressing problem."

"Okay," McFadden said. He ended the call and reached the courier again. "I'll be at your place in an hour."

"But I don't—"

"Relax, you're still getting paid. Don't go anywhere."

Steve Dane cleared customs and collected a small single suitcase before finding a taxi. He told the driver, "Downtown."

He'd never been to Istanbul before and he made this first visit alone. Nina had left Italy for Paris to look into a man named Daudet that Lukavina said was somehow connected to the Duchess.

He glanced at the photo as the taxi let him off in the square. The picture showed a young man walking in public. It was the only picture the CIA had of the courier. Finding the man wouldn't be easy, but there were ways if one had even an ounce of patience. He blended with the crowd. The warm summertime air meant most folks were dressed in light colors and loose-fitting items. Dane was no different. He wore tan khakis and a white long-sleeved shirt and leather jacket.

He stepped into an alley, kneeling with his case on the grimy concrete. From the X-ray-proof bottom he took out his Detonics, which he dropped into an inside pocket of his jacket. Rising with case in hand, he continued nosing around and finally spotted the limping courier traveling along the sidewalk.

Dane stopped behind a street vendor's wheeled cart once the mousy man neared the café.

The vendor approached Dane, holding up a tapestry. "You buy, good deal," the vendor said, waving a hand over the abstract pattern. To Dane it looked like a bunch of circles haphazardly drawn.

"Not today."

"Very cheap. Fifty dollars."

"No."

"Forty-five dollars. Very good buy. Impress your friends."

Dane waved the man off and stepped around the cart, and watched the man light a cigarette and drop a matchbook. He saw the other man get up from his chair and retrieve the matchbook. Dane grinned. Sean McFadden. Working for the Duchess? It had been a long time since their paths had crossed. Obviously, he was here to kill the courier. Dane watched the assassin walk off in the other direction. He followed the courier.

The reason for the aborted contact was clear. News of the events in Mestre had filtered down the chain and now the Duchess's agents needed to scatter. But McFadden wouldn't just pack up and leave. The mousy man had no idea that there was a target on his back.

Dane peeked around the corner and watched the courier enter his room. The door shut, the lock clicked, and Dane advanced down the hall with the Detonics in his right hand. He kicked the door open. The courier, in the process of placing wallet and keys on a nightstand, jumped in surprise. Dane grabbed a fistful of the man's shirt, forcing him onto the bed. He jammed the .45 into his neck.

"You like breathing?"

The courier rasped out some words.

"Tell me who the Duchess is."

The courier moved his mouth, but nothing came out.

Dane stepped back. He kept the courier covered while he shut the door. The man lay gasping, rubbing his neck. Dane patted him down for weapons but found none.

"Get your shoes off," he said.

The courier frowned.

"Now!"

The courier let the tennis shoes plop onto the floor. If he had any weapons concealed within, he couldn't use them now. The courier sat on the bed looking at Dane.

"You're working for the Duchess."

The courier nodded. "Yes."

"Tell me who she is."

"I don't know."

"Wrong answer."

"I swear I don't know! I've never seen her! I only work with her representatives! I'm telling the truth, don't kill me."

Dane said, "The man you were supposed to meet is coming here to kill you."

Beads of sweat broke out on the courier's forehead.

"I'm the only chance you have, kid," Dane said.

"But you'll kill me too!"

"Wrong. Who is the Duchess?"

"I don't know!"

"Then why does she want you dead?"

The courier stuttered a string of words. He raised a hand to wipe his face, but Dane gestured with his gun and the courier dropped his hand.

Dane clenched his teeth. This was a dead end. Pretty soon the kid would start whimpering and blubbering. The kid let out half a scream before Dane smacked him over the head and he fell over. Dane stretched him out and moved to the wall beside the door. Sean McFadden would arrive any minute. Perhaps Dane's old friend would be more willing to share words.

Dane laughed. Of course, he wouldn't.

Chapter Fifteen

McFadden hiked up the sloping sidewalk to the rooming house, a six-story stone building sandwiched between two other stone buildings in a street made up of more stone buildings. The Turks had come up with one way of construction back in the day and repeated it everywhere, though their modern efforts were a sight to see and a testament to architectural genius. McFadden went up the front steps, entered the small lobby and did not acknowledge the fat man at the front counter as he hustled up more steps to the courier's floor.

In the hallway McFadden took out the Walther PPQ and snapped off the safety. He held the compact pistol beside his right leg. At the courier's door, he knocked twice.

The knob turned and the door squeaked opened. McFadden stopped at the sight before him. The courier asleep on his bed with his shoes off. Who had opened the door? He stepped in and froze when the cold muzzle of a gun touched his neck.

"Hello, Sean," Dane said. "Is that the new Walther?"

"Latest and greatest for me," the assassin said. "I'll

leave the antiques to you."

"Drop the gun. Now."

McFadden released his hold on the Walther and dropped it on the carpet. He kicked it away. It stopped near the bed.

"Hands up."

The assassin raised his hands. "What are you doing here?"

"I'm looking for the Duchess."

"If she wants to see you, she will find you."

"Tell me where she is."

"No."

"Tell me *who* she is."

"No."

"You're going to stand here with my gun in your neck and not tell me anything?"

The courier stirred, moaned.

McFadden said, "You still hit like a girl."

"I wasn't really trying."

"Do you remember the first lesson you taught me?" McFadden said.

"You mean you actually paid attention?"

McFadden flung his right arm out to his side. A long tube slid down his sleeve and stopped in the palm of his hand; a flick of the wrist and the tube extended into a long metal baton. McFadden whirled, swinging. Dane brought up his left arm to block the blow and pressed the .45 into McFadden's chest. The assassin swept the baton upward, striking Dane's wrist. The gun did not fire but flew out of Dane's hand. Dane responded with kicks and punches. McFadden deflected some. The ones that landed against his hard body made him grunt. He slashed the baton from side to side, Dane jumping back. Dane grabbed a chair and lunged. McFadden swung, breaking the chair's legs.

They fell onto the carpet. Dane threw the chair. McFadden batted the chair away. Dane grabbed one of the fallen legs and launched his own attack, McFadden blocking with the baton, the awkward sword fight carrying them across the carpet. McFadden kicked Dane in the stomach. Dane bit off his scream. McFadden charged again, swinging the baton, clashing again with Dane's chair leg.

The courier rolled off the bed and grabbed the fallen Walther PPQ. He aimed at McFadden's back.

The courier awoke slowly, listening to the grunts and crashing, and as his eyes focused on the gun on the carpet. He saw his opportunity. He grabbed the gun. He aimed at the back of his contact, the man who had orders to kill him.

But the contact shifted before the courier fired. When he did pull the trigger, the gun bucked once, twice. One shot hit the wall; another cracked through the window behind the man who'd said he was there to help. McFadden whirled, charging at him, swinging the baton. The courier yelled and fired two more times but missed. McFadden swung and knocked the pistol from his grip. It crashed against the wall. The courier brought his smashed hand to his chest, gripping it with the other, howling. McFadden pivoted again, swinging at Dane, keeping him back, and then raced out through the open door.

"Nice shooting, jackass," Dane said before he ran out after the other man. He pounded down the hallway after McFadden. "Stop, Sean!"

McFadden crashed through the stairwell door. Dane reached the door as it swung closed. He shoved through, starting for the steps. A swoosh of air behind him. He turned just as the baton flashed past where his head had been. He brought up the .45, but the assassin struck with a backspin kick. Dane, who had nothing but the steps behind him, tumbled end over end. He crashed hard on the landing below, the wind knocked out of him, his head spinning, his whole body screaming.

McFadden plowed past him. His pounding boots echoed up and down the stairwell, faded away.

Dane stared at the brown spots on the ceiling for a long time. When he could breathe normally again, he climbed to his feet. Using the banister for support, he climbed the steps back to the hallway and returned to the courier's room.

The mousy man remained sitting on his bed. He blinked when Dane entered.

"Are you positive you don't know anything?" Dane said. "You've never seen the Duchess before?"

The courier shook his head.

"Grow eyes in the back of your skull, Einstein," Dane said, and left again. He kept a hand on one wall so he wouldn't fall over.

"I'm not pleased," the Duchess said.

"The odds changed, luv," McFadden said. "I haven't survived this long by being stupid."

The assassin sat in a leather chair on board a Lear jet, a private plane owned and operated by a front company owned by the Duchess. A glass of Bushmills, no ice, sat on the table beside him. The low hum of the engine did not overpower the woman's voice over McFadden's cell phone.

"Just get to Paris," she said. "Instructions await you there. Sean?"

"Yes, ma'am?"

"Don't miss."

Chapter Sixteen

Paris
Two Days Later

The reception for the new season of the Paris Opera, held in the
Grand Foyer of the Palais Garnier, one of the largest and
most beautifully built opera houses in all of France, was in
full swing. The three-tiered Grand Staircase overlooked the
festivities, the guests surrounded by the gold and marble
and long tapestries. The ceiling above, painted blood red
and white, was as dazzling as the rest of the foyer. The
guests of honor and the attendees were in for quite a night.

Dane, decked out in a black tuxedo with a jacket that
had not been tailored to hide a gun, wasn't a fan of the
opera. He knew better than to say so to Nina, who was
dressed in a strapless blue gown that hugged her figure but
left her shoulders bare. Her long black hair was tied back,
and her ponytail dangled just below her shoulder blades.
Only her tiger eyes, which scanned everything and missed
nothing, suggested that she was not one of the lesser mortals in attendance. Nina's mother had often brought her to

the Moscow opera when she was a child. As an adult, she never tired of the spectacle.

"What do you think?" she said to him.

"About what?"

"The show."

"What show?"

She shook her head and drank champagne. "One of these days I will teach you to appreciate fine things."

He grabbed her around the waist and pulled her to him. Her big eyes widened. "Not here," she said.

"I already appreciate the only fine thing I need." He nibbled her earlobe. She shoved him away, glancing around, brushing the side of her gown. Dane laughed.

The pair stood within earshot of the client.

Dane said, "We're out of leads if this is a dead end."

"I'm not sure it is," Nina said. "Daudet is under surveillance."

"How do you know that?"

"Because I watched the men trailing him," she said. "My idea was to initiate a field contact and see if Daudet would get spooked and call this Duchess person, but when I saw the surveillance team, it made me think again."

"You think he's a target?"

"I think somebody wants to take him out, yeah."

"How does that match what Lukavina told us?"

"I think we're going to find out soon enough," Nina said.

"Len would have told us if CIA was watching him."

"I didn't get the impression that was the case either."

Dane nodded. There was no reason to second-guess Nina. She knew the tradecraft as well as him. "What do I need to know about this guy?"

"He's the president and CEO of a cosmetics firm."

"Now I'm really confused. How in the world does

that connect him with an arms dealer trying to sell a nuclear bomb?"

Dane looked over at Nicholas Daudet, a man who stood proud but whose eyes reflected an inner melancholy. About six feet, with white hair. He stood with both hands behind his back while chatting with a fat lady in a poufy gold gown. Dane noted that it wasn't the fat lady who closed out the opera.

Next to Daudet, Nina explained, stood his oldest son, Alexis.

"Over there is the daughter."

Dane followed Nina's gaze to a young woman joined at the hip to her male companion. The woman's lush black hair, dark eyes and creamy complexion were her most alluring features. She had squeezed her rotund body into a black cocktail dress. The strap over her right shoulder had slipped off, yet she made no effort to correct the malfunction as she basked in the gaze of the young man who held her hands and seemed to be leading her in some sort of dance, the music for which seemed to flow from their fluttering love-struck hearts.

Dane wanted to gag at the sight.

"That's Solange," Nina said.

"And the man thing?"

"Fernand Martel. Works at a bakery. They've been dating for about two months."

"A rich man's daughter hangs out with a wage slave?"

"He doesn't like the boy."

"I don't like him, either. Too slick," he said, noting the designer shirt and slacks, his greased hair. Skinny, with prominent cheekbones and a jutting chin. "Looks like a crook. He doesn't belong here. He belongs in an alley with a switchblade waiting for a sucker to walk by."

"It's the twenty-first century, honey. Muggers use stun guns nowadays. He's okay."

"You sure?"

"I checked him out. He has a birth mark on his rear end." She grinned and nudged Dane with an elbow.

Dane ignored her. "What about the youngest son?"

"That would be Gerard. He's over there by himself. He hardly says a word to anybody, ever."

She pointed at a young kid who stood against a wall holding a glass of champagne that, judging by the fluid level, he had not sipped; he looked around with a glazed expression. Blonde hair, about twenty pounds overweight, one hand in a pocket. He kept shifting his weight to one leg or the other.

"There's a kid," Dane said, "with a lot on his mind."

"He'd rather be home playing video games," Nina said.

Dane looked around at the party guests. "Do any of these people look like assassins to you?"

"Not one."

He excused himself and wandered through the crowd, checking out the scene from different sides of the room. Nobody paid attention to him; nobody had the eyes of a hunter stalking a target; a look over at Daudet revealed that the fat lady in her gown was still babbling and Daudet was shooting pleading glances at his son Alexis, who was too tied up in a conversation with a skinny brunette with a tattoo down the center of her back to pay attention to the old man.

Presently the party finally broke up and the crowd flowed out into the cool night, some to waiting limos, the rest to the valet garage across the street. Dane and Nina discreetly followed the Daudet family down the steps. He scanned the crowd but saw no threat. Cars in the street crept by. A shooter could fire from one of those cars, but there was no promise of a clear line of fire. The Daudets' driver had the rear doors of their limo open. He looked at the garage across the street, scanning the levels and rooftop. That's where he would hide if he was a sniper. The rooftop was unlit, so no silhouette showed against the night sky. But then a flash winked in the dark. Dane yelled a warning and tackled Nicholas Daudet as somebody behind let out a scream. The echo of the shot came next.

Chapter Seventeen

Dane pressed the older man into the sidewalk. Daudet's wind whooshed out of him. The man squirmed underneath Dane and tried to push himself up; Dane forced him back down. "Stay!" More screaming, people rushing, shoes and heels scraping the pavement; somebody started yelling for police.

Nina shouted, "Gerard's hit!"

Dane looked back. The rest of the family had dived for cover behind the front pillars of the opera house, but Nina lay atop Gerard, who was bleeding, his face twisted in agony.

"Get in the limo!" Dane shouted, hauling the elder Daudet to his feet, despite the man's protests, forcing him to stay bent at the waist as he shoved him into the back seat. He helped gather Gerard while Nina ushered the others forward. As Dane loaded Gerard into the limo, he noticed there had been no follow-up shots. Nina went in last. She pulled the door shut. Dane jumped back as the driver screeched into traffic.

Dane ran across the street, dodging stopped cars, and raced up the stairs of the parking structure. Once on the roof he saw a dark figure running. He ran after the shoot-er, his shoes crunching the loose gravel strewn across the roof. The rooftops of the surrounding buildings resem-bled an oddly shaped alien landscape. The sniper turned and fired from the hip. The bullet whined over Dane's head. The sniper leapt from the edge of the roof to the neighboring building. Dane pounded across, jumped, and the hard shock of the landing jolted up his legs. The snip-er turned again. A mask covered the shooter's face. He fired another round, the projectile kicking up gravel near Dane's right foot.

The sniper threw down his rifle and drew a knife. Dane's momentum carried him into the sniper's body, and they crashed flat in a tangle of arms and legs. Dane rolled and lashed out with a kick, his foot swishing through air as the sniper rolled away and came up slashing, driving Dane back. Dane punched the other man, following up with a roundhouse kick that the sniper ducked. The sniper dived headfirst into Dane's midsection; the air rushed out of Dane's lungs as his back took the force of the landing. The sniper rose, jumping back. He held the knife in front of him but made no move to strike.

The sniper said, "We can do this all night if you want."

"Sean," Dane said through gritted teeth.

Sean McFadden pulled off the mask. The sweat on his face shined in the lights from the street. "I could have shot you all down there, you know."

The assassin laughed and took off running again and was gone.

Dane stood up, brushed off his clothes. His whole body hurt. He started back the way he came.

McFadden *again* meant the Duchess *for sure* and Dau-det was the target, not an accomplice. What did the man know and why did the Duchess want to kill him?

The answer would not be far away.

He made his way to the edge of the roof and looked down at the street. Police and emergency crews now dominated the boulevard. He could probably slip through the coverage, but just in case, he needed to be sans firearm. He unhooked the belt-clip holster from behind his back. The holster contained his Detonics .45, and he could not be caught with it. He did not intend to be caught, but one had to plan for bad hands as well as good. He placed it in a corner. Not the best hiding place, but it would do for now. Taking the stairs back to the sidewalk, he reached the street and had started to turn and walk away from the commotion when the beam of a flashlight lit him up.

"Stop! Hands up!"

Dane let out a long breath and raised his hands.

"He's bleeding all over!" Solange said.

"Keep pressure on the wound!" Nina told her.

"I can't!"

The limo jolted over a pothole. Gerard cried out.

The elder Daudet leaned across the space between the limo's bench seats and grabbed at Nina. "Who *are* you!?" he shouted.

Nina's glare sent the man back where he came from. "The only chance your family has of surviving!" Nina turned back to Solange. "Hold it like this!" She clamped a hand on the bundle of handkerchiefs she'd bunched together from everybody's outfits and Solange's purse, using the wad to try and stop Gerard's bleeding. The sniper had shot him between the neck and shoulder, just beneath the collarbone, but that didn't mean the collarbone hadn't shattered from the force of the impact. Nina wasn't an expert on wounds—all she knew for sure was that the boy was bleeding and needed medical attention fast. He couldn't stay still and twisted his body back and forth on the leather seat.

"Take it!" Nina said, removing her hand. The girl did as Nina had demonstrated. Nina glanced out the back window. Nobody was following them. The driver pressed the pedal to the floor and shouted that they were mere minutes from the hospital.

The elder Daudet sat against the door, his knees and elbows scrunched together, staring at the carpet. Not quite catatonic but not present, either. Alexis at least tried to keep his younger brother's body still while his sister covered the wound.

The driver screeched the limo to a stop in front of the emergency room. Nina jumped out and started yelling for a medic. When an orderly saw the blood spatter on her gown, he raced out. Nurses and a doctor followed. They unloaded Gerard and, placing him on a stretcher, wheeled him into the hospital. Nina guided the family inside, literally pulling Nicholas Daudet by the arm. Once inside, she shuffled them into a corner of the waiting room that wasn't occupied; other visitors across the room looked at them oddly. She could survive the looks but could not, alone, protect the group from another attack. But now that they were all inside the hospital, she could relax a little. Only a suicide attacker would dare a strike, and she didn't think their opponents were that type.

She found a seat and slipped off her heels and rubbed her feet. She wondered where Steve was.

Chapter Eighteen

The policeman set a cup of coffee on the table, but Dane did not touch it. Black coffee wasn't his thing. Especially police station black coffee.

He sat in a white-walled interrogation room with a single light burning above, handcuffed. He'd been there for three hours.

The man wore a dark suit and dark-rimmed glasses. He was older than most of the station cops Dane had seen so far and carried a weariness about him that he didn't bother to conceal. He said, "Mr. Dane, I am Inspector Jean-Louis Ambard."

"Good evening."

Ambard lit a cigarette and sat at the table. He blew a smoke ring. "I know your record, Mr. Dane," he said. "Interpol sent me some interesting tidbits, too. They think you're a criminal."

"Sure."

"But I don't."

"What gives you that idea?"

"There was an incident in Brussels last year. Something about a policeman's fiancée being kidnapped. Did you hear about it?"

"Maybe."

"Perhaps I am a friend of the family. You never know; it's a small world. I heard rumors…somebody helped the family, got the girl back, they lived happily ever after, all that. The family was very grateful. Maybe the policeman said something about it to me. I'm getting old, so I forget the details about things like that." He blew out another stream of smoke. "Listen. The Daudet kid came to me a few days ago and said that somebody wanted to hurt his father. I pressed him but he had no details. When I insisted he tell more, he turned white and clammed up, as you Americans say."

"You want something from me, Inspector."

"No, I simply make suggestions. You don't answer to me. But I do wield influence."

"Meaning?"

"You know how it is."

"Uh-huh."

Inspector Ambard said, "Daudet has given a statement through his lawyer."

"And?"

"He has confirmed your employment as a bodyguard because of threats against his life."

Nina works fast. "Uh-huh."

"Mr. Daudet's lawyer further demands that you either be released or charged. Charged with what, I really don't know. If somebody had fired from the roof, you would be perfectly within your duties to investigate. We have some very eager rookies today who want to be famous cops and have movies made about them. I don't understand them."

"Okay."

Ambard shrugged. "You are free to go, Mr. Dane." He unlocked the handcuffs and placed the steel bracelets on the table.

"I'm sure I'll see you again," the French policeman said. "And I hope it's not at the morgue."

Dane, rubbing his wrists, did not hide his grin. "You and me both."

"Daudet and his family are still at the hospital."

"How's the boy?"

"You'll have to ask his father."

Nina, barefoot and leaning against a wall with her arms folded, smiled when Dane entered the waiting room. She went over to him. "Okay?"

"Yes. Gerard?"

"In surgery."

"Prognosis?"

"Don't know."

Dane let out a breath. Nina moved behind him and kneaded his shoulders. "Where were you?"

"Police station."

"Did they beat you with a rubber hose?"

"No. There's an inspector named Ambard that I think we can trust," he said. He looked around. "Interesting scene here."

Nina said softly, "It's a soap opera."

Nicholas Daudet paced on one side of the room, hands kept in the pockets of his black trousers; head bowed, apparently tracing the cracks in the tiled floor.

Nina dug deeper into Dane's neck and shoulders. She said, "He was near catatonic in the car after I yelled at him. The kids tried to help Gerard while he wanted to argue with me. Then I had to half drag him in here. They took the kid into surgery, and he got on the phone, first to his lawyer, then to clients and partners."

"He told his lawyer to spring me."

"You're welcome."

"He talked to you?"

"He said we saved his life, yet he didn't know who we were, so I told him, and said you'd be along as soon as you could."

"Who is he talking to now?"

"Business associates. He changes gears very quickly. He's not telling them about Gerard. He hasn't even mentioned it. He's working out details of a deal. He's doing business while we wait. Can you believe that?"

"When under stress he turns to work. Not terribly uncommon."

"But look around, Steve. This is hardly the time for that."

His older son, Alexis, sat alone on the far end of the row of chairs in the center of the waiting room. He was tapping the armrest and staring at a spot on the floor.

The daughter, Solange, leaning against boyfriend Fernand, sat across the room against the far wall.

"This family knows togetherness," Dane said.

"Did you see who was on the roof?"

"See him? I trained the sucker."

"Do tell."

"He and I used to work together. Sean McFadden."

"The IRA shooter."

"Ex. He quit the cause after the Dayton agreements."

"He must have been—"

"A kid then, yeah. I recruited him for 30-30 and taught him a few things."

"But now he's free-lance."

"And a good sniper. Too good for what happened

tonight."

"Working for the Duchess?" Nina said.

"Yes. I tangled with him in Istanbul, too."

"He gets around."

"Forget that for now. Ambard says Gerard visited him and said somebody was going to try and hurt his father," Dane said. "I don't see how taking him out would help."

"There's a reason," she said. "Always is."

"Of course."

"What will we do next?"

Before Dane could answer, Daudet came over. He stopped, threw back his shoulders and regarded Dane like a general inspecting a line of troops.

"You saved our lives," Daudet said.

"You already said that," Nina told him.

Daudet ignored her. "I am Nicholas Daudet."

"Steve Dane."

He acknowledged Nina with a glance, then turned back to Dane. "Why were you at the opera tonight?"

"You're in danger," Dane said.

"Why?"

"We're trying to find out."

"I am a simple businessman, Mr. Dane. Nobody shoots at people like me."

"There's a reason. We'll find it."

"Unless you're the ones who are going to do the shooting?"

Nina said, "I could have killed you all in the limo and you know it."

Daudet's eyes widened.

"Everybody take it easy," Dane said. "Especially you, Nina."

"Don't tell me—"

"Enough."

Nina stopped talking but a red flush crawled up her neck.

Daudet squared his shoulders. "Your actions spared the life of my son."

"The doctor—"

"I saw the wound before he went into surgery," Daudet said. "It is not a serious one."

"With all due respect—"

"I was in the war, Mr. Dane. I know gunshot wounds."

"Which—"

"Does it matter? There is always a war somewhere."

Dane nodded.

"What do you propose to do next?" the older man said.

"Well—"

"I want to go home as soon as I know Gerard will be okay."

Nina jumped in. "Home is hardly the place to be—"

"I want to go home, Miss Talikova."

Dane said to Nina, "Can you hold the fort for a few hours?"

"Not without help."

"Won't get here in time. A few hours, tops."

"Fine. I'll go back to the house while you prowl and growl, but don't be long." She fixed a glare at the older man.

"What does this 'prowl and growl' mean?" Daudet said, oblivious to Nina's gaze.

"You'll see when we get our claws on the man who shot your son," Dane said.

Daudet nodded and stepped away to get his family together.

"Catatonic?" Dane said.

"I could swear he was on another planet," she said. "He

sure is a punk, though."

"He's French, honey. They're born that way."

Nina mumbled a curse against Daudet's ancestors. "Are we going to tell him what's going on?" she said.

"I want to string him along a little," Dane replied. "Let's see how this develops."

The pair herded the Daudet family and Fernand back outside. Solange wanted Fernand to come back with them, but her father said no. Fernand said he would catch a cab back to his home, not far from the hospital.

"Call me tomorrow," Solange told him. They kissed and hugged, and Daudet yelled at her to get in the car. She watched Fernand from the back window as the driver accelerated away.

Nina watched the girl settle into her seat. She had been that young once, but before her mind drifted too far, she started scanning the areas outside the car for any other threats. The past wasn't meant to be thought about. Not hers, anyway.

Chapter Nineteen

The limo's insulation blocked out the road noise, so it was a quiet ride. The leather seats felt like Dane's couch, though he couldn't remember how long it had been since he had visited his Vienna domicile. The tinted windows obscured the passing scenery, but one countryside was the same as another, in his experience.

Nobody said a work or looked at anyone else. Only Dane and Nina exchanged occasional glances.

The driver steered the limo up the crescent driveway of the Daudet home. The three-story mansion, made of red brick with vines climbing the walls at various spots, occupied several acres, with trimmed grass and forest taking up the surrounding space. Nice place to hide, Dane decided, and a nice place for a battle nobody would hear, and the cops couldn't respond to until the bad guys were gone. He shook his head. As a hideout, it made a great death trap.

Once inside, Alexis and Solange retreated to their bedrooms. Dane conferred with Nicholas.

"I need—"

"My car. Of course."

"If you have an alarm, turn it up to eleven."

Daudet blinked. "What?"

"Never mind," Nina jumped in. "We got it covered, Steve."

"I have some clothes," Daudet said to Nina, "that might fit you. My late wife's things."

She said okay and accompanied Dane to the garage, where the Porsche waited. Dane whistled. The bright blue paint job glistened under the garage lights.

"Where are you going to start?" she said.

"A couple of friends might have something," he said.

"Who?"

"One of them is from the old outfit. He runs a bar."

"You said two. A couple is *two*."

Dane cleared his throat. "There's our old pal Anna Dalen," he said.

"Gun dealer. Runs around with that ex-Army guy."

"You remember."

Nina folded her arms and frowned. "I also remember you had a fling with her a long time ago."

Dane winked. "That was before you, sweetie."

"I don't want you seeing her."

"Honey, I have no choice. Otherwise we can't save the world."

She folded her arms and pressed her lips together and didn't acknowledge his peck on her cheek. Dane jumped behind the wheel and waved. Nina continued to fume.

He followed the winding roads with deftness, the boosted motor of the Porsche Turbo growling with each press of the accelerator. Dane couldn't fight the grin that spread across his face. It may have been the dreaded 996 variant, with its water-cooled engine and funky headlamps, but it had the magic that counted.

He crossed city limits. First stop: the building where he'd ditched his gun. He retrieved his pistol and returned to the car. Driving deeper into the city, he found another parking garage, slid the Porsche into an empty slot and hit the sidewalk.

He checked out the boutique restaurants and shops that lined the streets. Many of the restaurants offered outdoor seating, which narrowed walking space, and once or twice he had to step off into the street because of other pedestrians coming his way. He frowned at the sights, many of which had not existed when he last visited. The streets had been repaved, the sidewalks widened because of the outdoor dining spots, and a roundabout intersection sported a tall fountain in the center. When he arrived at the bar he wanted, the address was right, but the name was completely different.

The place had always been called *A Voie de Pirate*, the Pirate's Way. The neighborhood had not always been so posh, and the rough-and-tumble watering hole had fit right in. Now the sign read *Boisson Pour!*, or Drink Here! Odd name, Dane thought, but to the point, and the neon sign with its low glow flashed off and on. Piano music drifted out as a couple exited. Dane frowned. Something wasn't right. He went inside to find out.

The piano player sat on a raised stage in front of full tables and a full bar. Older clientele. Low light, dark-paneled walls and black-and-white checkered tile floor. Dane let out a breath. This was not the same place his pal Monty had owned. He and Monty went back to Dane's days as commander of the 30-30 Battalion. Monty had opened the bar with the considerable savings he'd accumulated during their years of adventures, but he could not stay out of the action. He kept up his contacts in the intelligence world, and in the underworld, and came in handy when fellow outlaws like Dane needed info.

Dane turned to leave, but as he did his eyes landed on a one-eyed parrot dangling above the piano. The parrot had a broken wing. He smiled. The parrot was the only indication of what had been there before. Monty still ruled the roost.

He found an empty table in a back corner. A blonde waitress kept passing him by as she busied about more visible tables. He finally leaned out and waved, and she came over.

He didn't need a menu. He ordered a sidecar. "Is Monty working tonight?"

She said yes.

"Tell him Steve is here."

The waitress went away and returned a few moments later with his drink, a yellowish mixture of Cointreau, cognac, lemon juice and a cherry, in a martini glass. The waitress said it was on the house and went away before Dane said anything more. He sipped the chilled concoction and let the sour warmth run into his belly.

A dark-haired woman in a long yellow dress joined the piano man and the bar hushed. She began singing a slow, mournful tune about heartbreak. Dane felt it. He started turning the glass in circles as his reflection carried him back to some fifteen years earlier, but before his vision of a particular summer solidified, a hulking figure in an ugly pea-green coat sauntered over. Dane jumped up with an extended hand.

"Steve!" They shook.

"Been a long time, Monty."

They sat.

"Like what I've done with the place?"

"I thought you were long gone. The parrot said otherwise."

"I insisted on keeping that. My investors disagreed, said it would ruin the image, but they knew if I pulled out, they would lose the place, so they let me keep him there. Nobody complains."

"Investors?"

"The city wanted to improve the neighborhood, so I had to update. These other fellows wanted to buy into a club, so we worked out a deal. Everybody's happy."

"You're boring me."

Monty let out a hearty laugh.

"What brings you back here?" Monty said.

"Little bit of action tonight," Dane said, and told him about the Daudet adventure so far.

Monty was aware of the Duchess, but admitted her whereabouts, and a description, weren't something his contacts had acquired.

"What's the word on the street?" Dane said.

"Oh, that's easy. Sean isn't the only player here."

"Anybody else I might know?"

"Dumb muscle, mostly. And the Duchess has something major going on either in Paris or nearby, but I don't know what that is."

"Or where?"

"Exactly. But one of our favorite people is tied up in it."

"Which one?"

"Leo Gordov."

"How about that. He's been quiet for ten years," Dane said, "and now he shows up? I bet he ran out of money."

"Your guess is as good as anything else. He's guilty of many crimes. There is still a large bounty on his head."

"How much?"

"One million from the Americans and two million pounds from the British. Dead or alive."

"Where is he?"

"Don't know."

"You're not much help, Monty."

"There is another friend of ours who may know."

"Anna Dalen, I know. I was going to look her up next."

"She and Dan Hunter have been poking around a lot. She doesn't want the Duchess moving in on her clientele."

"She still thinks of others first, how nice," Dane said. "I'd ask where they're staying, but you probably don't know."

Monty grinned. "That I do know, my friend."

"Forget it. Anna always had this odd habit of finding me before I could find her."

Chapter Twenty

Steve Dane turned right as he exited the bar, Monty's words bouncing to and fro through his mind. No answers, but more pieces of the puzzle. Heavy footsteps behind him. Dane glanced back. Two men in dark clothes, seemingly caught up in a chat, but Dane saw their eyes shift his way. He walked a block, sidestepping open eating areas; he looked back while covered by a lamppost and saw one of the shadows talking into a phone. On the surface it was nothing. Dane wasn't going to bet on that.

Traffic, momentarily stopped by a red light, started to move. Dane bolted into the street, forcing cars to stop. As horns assailed him, he reached the other side, cut around a corner and looked back. The man with the phone was still talking, but they were heading his way. Dane started moving again, passing shops and bars. Another man, this one alone, dressed like the other two shadows, moved with the crowd ahead and before Dane collided, he slipped into a sandwich shop.

The line of customers at the counter didn't notice him at first; the five sandwich makers, taking orders, didn't notice him, either. Soup simmered on a stove somewhere. The appetizing scent of French onion tickled his nose. He aimed for the employee door at the end of the counter and shoved through. Then somebody did notice him. The owner, grabbing wrapped loaves of bread from a rack, turned, gaped. He charged at Dane, a loaf in each hand, waving the bread like weapons. "Get out of here!"

Dane ducked under the owner's swinging arm, jabbed him in the solar plexus. The owner let out a rush of air and staggered aside. Dane kept going, winding through the back stockroom, stepping over a small pile of produce that had apparently fallen, the owner yelling at his back with a strained voice. He pushed through the alley door and let it slam shut.

A silenced gunshot blasted a chunk of brick, and the shards pelted Dane's face. Dane dropped and rolled across the alley floor, over a patch of wet garbage, to the cover of a dumpster. Running footsteps echoed. He rolled from cover with the .45 in hand and fired twice. The third shadow jerked with each hit. His momentum carried him forward, and he fell inches from Dane's face.

More scraping footsteps at six o'clock. Dane rolled onto his back. The first two tails converged. Dane fired high, his shot ricocheting off a wall. The two men flattened out. Dane leapt up and ran with silenced shots popping at his heels. He fired one shot over his shoulder. The crack of the unsilenced pistol bounced off the alley walls. As he neared the mouth of the alley, a convertible screeched to a stop, blocking the way. A man with sandy hair and a long leather jacket whipped up an Uzi machine pistol. Dane dropped and rolled as the Uzi chattered, but the 9mm stingers landed nowhere near him.

The driver, a dark-haired woman with her long hair

tied back, the outline of her jaw prominent on her thin face, shouted, "Jump in, Steve!" Dane sprang for the car and vaulted into the passenger seat. The woman accelerated into traffic.

Dane looked at the sandy-haired man with the smoking Uzi pistol. The man dropped the weapon and slapped Dane on the shoulder. "You owe me one."

Dane grinned at Dan Hunter, turning an eye to the driver, Anna Dalen. He said, "Nick of time, Anna."

"I'm here to help."

Hunter chimed in. "Chasing you was like following a bouncing ball."

"You mean my stealth tactics were for nothing?"

"We need to have a long talk," Anna said.

"I hear we're in town for the same thing. Where to?"

Anna made a sharp right turn. "Our hotel," she said.

The countryside is nice only during the day, Nina decided. At night it was spooky. Nina patrolled the outer area of the Daudet home with a flashlight in one hand and her Smith & Wesson M&P Shield in the other.

No fence surrounded the property, which sat in the center of several acres. At the edge of the acreage was a line of trees. She shined the light on the bushes, around the stone sculpture in front of the home, and crossed the damp grass to the tree line. She lit the darkness with the bright beam. A twig snapped to her left. She turned that way, dropping low and scooting for cover. She aimed her light at an outline of motion and caught the back side of a figure running away. Killing the light, Nina stretched out on her belly, slowed her breathing. Were there more? Only the wind and the rustle of leaves and branches filled the otherwise silent night. Whoever the figure was, he'd come alone. A scout, maybe. For how many?

She stood up and brushed off her shirt. The jeans and T-shirt she had changed into upon arrival beat the heck out of her gown.

Nina re-entered the house. Most of the lights were out. A door shut somewhere; she turned left down a hall, shining the light. A line of light glowed under a doorway. Nina turned off the flashlight and stood there. A toilet flushed, water ran in a sink, and presently the door opened. Nina flashed the light. Alexis Daudet, in his bathrobe, blocked the flash with an arm.

"Is that necessary?" he said.

Nina lowered the light. "I saw somebody outside. I thought he might have broken in."

"Nobody has broken in."

"Why are you down here?"

"Because my bedroom," Alexis said, "is right *there*," and he pointed further along the hall to an open door.

Nina said okay. He's as big an ass as his father. Alexis grumbled and returned to the room. Advancing further down the hall, she found a locked door that, when opened, led to the side yard. She shined the light on the brick steps and saw a patch of mud on the middle part. She went into the bathroom, shining the light around, and caught another bit of mud in a corner where it might have dropped after the shoe that had brought it in was hastily removed.

Could Alexis have been spying on her?

She followed the beam of light back down the hallway to the one lighted room—the television room. Solange Daudet sat on one of the large leather couches facing a wide-screen TV showing a music video. She muted the show as Nina joined her. She sank into the large cushions. She set the gun and flashlight on the carved oak coffee table in front of the couch.

"Everything outside okay?"

"I'd feel better if we had ten or twenty other guys on watch."

Solange's big brown eyes widened.

"Don't worry, we'll be fine."

"How do you know?"

"This isn't my first trip to the rodeo," she said.

"The what?"

"Never mind."

Solange said, "I wish Dad hadn't insisted on coming here."

"Your father is looking for a comfort level. It's the way a lot of people deal with shock or a sudden change in life. They want something familiar close by so things don't seem so out of control. For your father, it's this house."

She wanted to say his family should have been enough to fill the psychological requirement, but after what she'd witnessed at the hospital, it was too much to suggest.

Solange said, "You know something about that yourself, don't you?"

Nina nodded.

"How did you handle it?"

"Never mind. Anything to drink in this house? Glass of wine, maybe?"

Solange stood up. "I prefer vodka."

"That will work, too."

Chapter Twenty-One

Nina lost count of how many glasses they had polished off. The bottle was more than halfway gone, though. They made the usual rounds of girl talk about clothes and movies and makeup and food and men and men again, and finally Nina said, "How old are you?"

"Twenty-three."

"I think I was that age once."

"What do you mean?"

"A lot of things happen," Nina said, "that make you forget where you came from. But we mustn't dwell on the past."

She swallowed more vodka and let it burn down her throat and warm her belly. *Twenty-three.*

Her eyes darted left and right, her neck and shoulders tightening; the usual fight-or-flight response she felt whenever Steve wasn't around. A lithe, feral cat. But there was nobody here to harm her. She knew that. Right now, anyway. That could change, and she had to be ready. She wanted to blame too many years of field work, but that would have been a lie. She could trace her anxiety to one freezing Moscow night under the Zhivopisny Bridge when she was twenty-three years old, the same age as Solange, fighting the chill off the Moskva River, while men with guns hunted for her.

She had been out on a date with her boyfriend at the time, crossing the bridge to the midway point to look at the dark river below as it rippled and slapped against the concrete walls on either side that had been built to contain the water while Moscow grew up around it.

Dimitri had been babbling all night about his acceptance for an investigator's position at the FSB after spending a few years as a Moscow beat cop. Dimitri wanted to see Russia return to its glory days as a world power. Protecting her interests from the inside seemed like a good way to help, what with all the corruption and blatant abuse by the elites taking place all over the country. To Nina, it had been too much to think about, so she hadn't. But Dimitri thought a lot about it.

They stood on the bridge and listened to the water and watched the lights of the city, and then Dimitri's grip on her tightened. A trio of men approached from the left side of the bridge, and Dimitri told her to run. "Run, fast! Run, now!" Before she cleared the span, the pops of gunfire destroyed the tranquility of the night, and she turned to watch Dimitri fall as the bullets ripped through him, his own pistol discharging uselessly as he landed. The trio saw her. She turned to run again.

She managed to elude them in the park on the other side of the bridge, taking advantage of the trees and shadows and swimming back across the Moskva to where Dimitri had left his car.

It didn't take long to learn that Dimitri had been making inquiries on his own time regarding a local Mafia chief, who ultimately decided that snuffing a junior officer was worth the trouble and time.

Later, Nina met a man named Alek Savelev, who saw her desire for vengeance and showed her how to get it. But there had been consequences to the act that still gave her nightmares. Shortly after, she'd met Dane. After that, there was no reason to stay in Russia.

"How long have you known Steve?"

Nina blinked a few times as Solange stirred her from the memories. "Couple years," she said. "We met in Montenegro. He was trying to steal some jewels that I wanted to bring back to my country. They belonged to my country, actually. Ever hear of Princess Anastasia? They were supposedly some of her jewels. But they were fakes. And instead of jewels, I caught Steve and only went back home long enough to resign from the FSB."

"What's that?"

"Russian federal police. Used to be the KGB, and they still are. In Russia, all we do is change the letters around but nothing else changes."

"What made you join them?"

"What did I tell you about the past? I want to talk about now. Now I travel the world with a handsome man, and we cause all kinds of trouble. Good ol' Stevie."

"Sounds like fun."

"Not always."

"Why?"

"One hotel room after another sounds fun? Often I wake up and wonder where I am." Usually after one of the nightmares.

"Don't you have a house or something?"

"Austria, just outside Vienna, but we aren't there much."

"In the Alps? I love skiing there."

"Near the Alps."

"What you describe is better than this place," Solange said. "I want to get away from this family. Fernand seems like the best ticket."

"Is that all he is to you?"

"Oh, I like him, but—you know. It's like you and Steve. Good ol' Stevie, you said."

"Don't misjudge me," Nina said.

"What?"

"Steve is not a ticket to anywhere except fun and excitement and romance and plenty of exotic locales, and hand me the bottle, child." Nina topped off her glass and set the bottle between them again.

"I would hate to see you waste your time and his," Nina said. "If you want to get out of here, that's okay, but don't link up with a stooge just because he's there."

"But what if—"

"If is a dangerous word," Nina said. "We shan't say it again tonight, okay?"

"Are you sure you should drink so much?"

"Don't worry. It takes more than a few glasses of vodka to spoil my aim."

Anna Dalen handed Dane a rum and Coke. She took a seat next to Dan Hunter on the couch opposite Dane. She'd untied her hair, and the unbrushed black mane, thick and wild, fell around her shoulders.

Hunter, sans leather coat, looked like a cowboy in his flannel shirt, jeans and boots. Appropriately enough, he was from Texas, but most of his accent had faded long ago—a casualty of living everywhere in the world but Texas.

Dane smiled as Anna scooted close to Hunter and he put an arm around her. They had not always been lovers. Hunter, a former major in the Army Criminal Investigations Division had once tried to arrest Anna for selling stolen US weapons; when the pursuit blossomed into a romance and the weapons in question were found in the possession of a terrorist instead of Anna, Hunter resigned from the Army and hooked up with her for good.

"You two look well," Dane said.

"Not so bad yourself," Anna said.

Dane had worked with Anna and Hunter many times; they had supplied him with weapons and other necessary equipment and even shelter when the heat was on.

"Where's Nina?" Hunter said.

Dane gave them a rundown of his activities in Paris so far; he filled them in on the events in Mestre and how he'd first learned about the Duchess.

"She's not wasting time with nickel-and-dime stuff," Hunter said. "A backpack nuke is serious hardware."

Dane saluted Hunter with his glass. "Quite the understatement, my friend."

"We hadn't heard of this," Anna said. "Our interest—"

"Is preserving your customer base?" Dane said.

"Gotta look out for number one," Anna said. "I'm the girl who sells guns, not this poser. And I certainly don't sell nukes to al-Qaeda. Even I have standards. Despite Dan." She gave him a playful nudge. He smiled.

Hunter said, "You probably just want to shoot her."

"Sure," Anna said.

"The thought had occurred to me as well," Dane said.

"But nobody knows where she is or what she looks like," Anna said.

Hunter said, "We do know that she's working with Leo Gordov."

"Monty mentioned that."

"He blew his retirement money, you know," Anna said.

"If by retirement money you mean what he made selling his services to the highest bidder," Hunter said. "Usually bad guys."

"Monty didn't know where Gordov was."

"Oh, we do," Anna said. "Would you like to join us for a little old-fashioned hammer party?"

Chapter Twenty-Two

Nina removed her bathrobe and left it on the carpet. The blue silk pajamas, also from the late Mrs. Daudet's wardrobe, were perfect, even if they didn't fit quite right. If she had to run out and engage the enemy, she didn't want her top or bottom or any other part of her body covered only by a wispy piece of lingerie.

The bedroom had a private bathroom and a double bed with a pillow top. Nice digs. The bedroom adjoined Solange's, and as Nina climbed into bed and turned off the lamp, she heard Solange's music thump-bumping through the wall. She stayed awake until the music switched off. Before she drifted off, she decided that the bed was nice but it would have been nicer with Steve to curl up with.

The gunshot jolted her awake. Before Solange screamed, she had her slippers on and the Smith & Wesson in hand. She shoved Solange's door open. The girl, sitting up in bed, screamed again, pointing out the shattered window. Nina went over, keeping to one side. Part of the roof and yard were visible; it would not have been hard for the shooter to climb up, but why shoot at Solange?

Nicholas and Alexis Daudet, sans robes, their PJs rumpled, ran in.

"What happened?"

"Somebody—"

"Are you hurt?" Daudet said to his daughter. Without leaving the doorway. Solange continued sobbing into her comforter.

Alexis wandered over to the window.

"Don't show yourself," Nina said.

"Please," Alexis said, peering through the hole. Further shots were not fired, and Alexis turned away with his face still intact. Nina could not decide if that was a tragedy or not.

She said, "We can't stay—"

"I will not be forced from my home," Daudet said.

"Then we need—"

"No police!"

"What the hell is your problem?"

"If you need help," Alexis said, "call Dane and tell him to come back."

"He's busy trying—"

"I told you in the beginning I wanted this handled discreetly," Daudet said.

"And your boyfriend," Alexis said, "has not checked in. Do you think he's dead?"

"I'd know."

"How?"

"Sixth sense."

Solange jumped off her bed and, shoving by her father, ran out of the room. Her father did not pursue. Nina followed, calling her name. Solange disappeared into the shadows at the end of the hall. Nina went downstairs and found the young woman in the kitchen, in a dark corner, with her knees up to her chin. She wasn't crying, but her unblinking thousand-yard stare broke Nina's heart.

Nina sat on the tiled floor beside the girl and put out an arm. Solange curled close.

"They don't care," she said.

Nina gave the girl a squeeze. "I care," she said.

Dane, Anna and Hunter were rigged for nighttime combat. Black clothes and boots, face paint, caps over their heads. Anna had offered Dane a weapon more potent than his Detonics, but he'd refused. Anna and Hunter went for heavier arms— Hunter his micro-Uzi and Anna an HK MP5K.

Anna picked the lock and pulled open the warehouse's alley door as Hunter shimmied down a phone pole. The warehouse alarm would have sent a signal to the cops via telephone line; Hunter had cut the circuit to avoid that hurdle.

Dane let Hunter enter after Anna and pulled the door shut behind them.

Each carried a flashlight, and the bright beams stabbed through the dark interior. They picked out stacks of crates against one wall; the rest of the warehouse was wide-open concrete floor.

"They wouldn't keep anything here, would they?" Dane said.

"We use fronts like this all the time," Anna said. "Who pays attention to warehouses?"

Dane's light landed on the window of a small office across the floor. He went that way while Anna and Hunter checked out the crates. The door beside the window wasn't locked. Dane entered and scanned the papers on the desk, peeked through bare filing cabinets, and flashed the light everywhere looking in vain for anything that even looked like a clue.

He rejoined Anna and Hunter, who had popped one of the crates open. Inside were cardboard boxes. Hunter removed one box; Dane slit it open with a knife. In the box were individually packaged bottles of Passion Flower, Daudet's best-selling perfume.

Nobody said a word. They kept pulling out boxes until they reached a compartment containing three automatic rifles. They were US M-16A2s, possibly from the cache reportedly stolen by the Duchess.

"A piece of the puzzle?" Hunter said.

"Maybe," Dane said. "The CIA says she's trying to move some US inventory. This might be it. Where's it going?"

A vehicle rumbled up the alley, the brakes squeaking as the machine stopped. Doors opened and closed.

Dane, Anna and Hunter ducked around the side of the crates. The side door they'd entered through did not swing out; instead another door, out of sight, opened. Two men exchanged words, their voices growing louder; they rounded the corner and entered the office. They snapped on a light and illuminated part of the open floor.

"Know them?" Dane said.

Both Anna and Hunter shook their heads.

The two men did not stop talking, and their voices echoed through the warehouse.

"If we stay in the shadows, we can get out of here," Hunter said.

Dane covered the lit office with his .45 as Hunter and Anna moved out, staying away from the spill of light. They reached the alley door and waited. Dane's shoes brushed the concrete as he ran. Hunter shoved open the door, and the trio gained the blacktop outside.

Somebody shouted.

Up the alley sat an SUV with a man leaning against the bumper, smoking. He hollered again and reached behind his back. A burst from Hunter's micro-Uzi drove the man to cover; he was still yelling as the trio piled into Anna's convertible. The motor fired with a single twist of the key, and she peeled off into the night.

Chapter Twenty-Three

It took about an hour to calm Solange enough to get her back into bed, but no further incidents disturbed the house.

Until everybody woke up in the morning anyway.

When Nina finally arose, the first thing she saw was a text from Steve on her cell: *Safe. Be in touch soon.*

She spit out a curse. This house wasn't safe. She had to get them out somehow. She showered and dressed and went downstairs, where Nicholas Daudet sat reading the paper.

"Where—"

"Alexis has gone for a walk," Daudet said, bifocals gripping the edge of his nose, "and Solange remains asleep."

"She deserves it." Nina entered the kitchen with a triumphant grin. She'd actually completed a sentence in front of the man! But seeing him engrossed in the newspaper told her he hadn't been listening anyway.

She finished her second cup of coffee, and Solange still had not come down.

Nina made a circuit of the grounds, noting footprints in the grass from the overnight shooter. He'd scraped part of

the outside wall when he'd climbed to Solange's window.
There were no footprints anywhere else. The shooter had
gone straight for Solange's window.

Why her? Alexis had a bedroom on the ground floor.
Why was he not a target, too?

And how did the shooting relate to Alexis's sneaking
around the grounds, like she suspected?

Nina went upstairs to the girl's bedroom and found
the bed empty.

Daudet was still reading his newspaper when she went
back downstairs.

"Solange is gone. Did you see her leave?"

The older man looked up with only a frown.

Nina ran to the garage and found the girl's car gone.
She told Daudet.

"Where did she go?" the father demanded.

Nina shook her head and grabbed the keys to another car.

Daudet said, "You can't leave me alone!"

Nina tossed him her pistol. He tried to catch it, fumbled,
and the gun dropped on his left foot. He glared at her. She
went out.

Yes, she was abandoning her principal. But she couldn't
abandon Solange too.

She remembered where she used to run when home
turned rough, and it gave her an idea of where Solange had
disappeared to. Solange would go to Fernand's. She tried
his home first and was told he was at work. She went to the
bakery. Nina entered the small white-walled establishment
and saw Solange at a corner table munching a croissant.
She stopped chewing and turned guilty eyes on Nina.

"Please don't be mad at me," Solange said as Nina
sat down.

"We have to go."

"I didn't mean—"

Nina held up a hand. "I know. Come on."

Nina and Solange scraped back their chairs; as Nina turned for the door, Fernand, a flour-covered apron wrapped around his clothes, swung around the counter and blocked the way.

"You can't take her," he said.

"Out of my way."

"Fernand—"

"No. You'll be safe with me."

"Move. Now."

Fernand folded his arms.

Nina socked him on the chin. He spun to one side but did not fall. Nina grabbed Solange by the hand and hauled her out of the bakery.

Anna steered the convertible into the parking garage, where Dane had left Daudet's Porsche Turbo. She stopped behind the German sports car.

"Hope you had fun," Anna said.

"We have to do this again sometime," Hunter said from the back.

"I have a feeling we will," Dane said, "and very soon." He told them good-bye and climbed out, digging the keys to the Porsche out of a pocket.

Anna made a U-turn, her tires screeching on the smooth garage floor, and shot away with a final wave.

Dane unlocked the Porsche. It had been a long night on Anna's couch, and his back was sore. The warehouse discovery still burned brightly in his mind's eye. It wasn't hard to figure out the entire scheme.

He pulled the driver's door open.

"Stop."

Dane went for the Detonics .45, but Sean McFadden already had him covered with his Walther. He stood near a concrete support beam about 20 feet away and held the gun close to his body. It was still early enough that there were only a few scattered cars in the garage, but bystanders could come through at any time. Dane didn't want to fool around. He placed both hands on the roof of the car.

"Take your gun out and kick it away."

"Stop it, Sean. Put yours away. Somebody's going to see us."

McFadden approached the Porsche and stopped near the back-quarter panel.

"There's no reason for you to be doing this, Sean."

"I'm doing a job, just like you."

"Quit."

"And join the ranks of the virtuous?"

"You don't have to work for people like the Duchess," Dane said.

"If I don't stay under the radar, I'm finished, old friend. I'm wanted by the British government. Bloody maggots want to hang me. If I start turning up in polite company, it means my neck. Besides, I've never been very polite."

"They have other fish to fry. You can give them those fish. Turn over what they want, and they'll forget about you really quick."

"Bit of a problem with that, luv," McFadden said. "What was that one bit of wisdom you taught that was so important to you?"

Dane sighed. "Don't cheat your client." He clenched his jaw. "Now what?"

"I'm not here to kill you, luv," McFadden said. "Somebody wants to see you, so let's go. We'll take my car."

McFadden drove a route not unfamiliar to Dane, and presently parked in the side alley beside the warehouse. He escorted Dane into the office, where a man sat behind the desk. Two gunmen stood in there with him.

McFadden shoved Dane inside. "Here he is."

"Are you staying?" the man behind the desk said.

"Got other orders, luv," McFadden said. He put the Detonics on the desk. "Don't let him have that." The Irishman turned to leave.

"Sean?" Dane said.

McFadden turned back.

"The next time I see you will be the last time."

"This *is* the last time," McFadden said, and departed.

Dane faced the man behind the desk.

"I will show you a sign of respect, Mr. Dane, and not restrain you. I trust you won't let me down."

Dane approached the desk. When the goons took a step forward, he stopped. He said, "This is usually the part where I'm tied to a chair and you whack my balls with a carpet beater so I suppose I'll save us all some time and effort and cooperate."

"I may have you beaten yet, Mr. Dane," said the other man. He smiled. Leo Gordov had perfect white teeth. The paunchy former Russian colonel still had a thick mop of hair, but his trimmed beard showed spots of gray.

Dane said, "You vanished after Tripoli."

"There was somebody who came very close to putting a bullet in my head."

Dane shrugged. "I'm sorry I missed. But you should have saved your money."

"You know how it is. There's always more money somewhere, you just have to go find it."

"What's on your mind?" Dane said.

"I want to know where Daudet is."

"At his country house."

"No, he isn't. That place was empty when we showed up an hour or so ago."

Dane shrugged. "You'll have to ask Nina. She must have made them move without telling me. I was on my way back there, actually, when Sean showed up."

Gordov sighed and rubbed his face with a fleshy palm. He said, "Break something," to one of the goons. The thug on his left grabbed Dane's left hand as the right-side goon clamped a thick arm around Dane's neck and squeezed. Dane choked off a grunt, his windpipe feeling the pressure of the squeeze.

Dane lashed out with one leg and kicked the first thug in the groin. The big man doubled over, little noises escaping his lips, face glowing red. Dane braced himself accordingly and flipped the second goon over his back. The second man landed on top of the first. The thug tried to rise. Dane kicked the side of his jaw and put him out.

Gordov grabbed the Detonics from the desk and lifted the gun to fire at Dane, who grabbed the pistol by the slide, twisting hard. Gordov screamed as his wrist turned with the twist. He released the pistol and dropped back into his chair, holding his right arm tight against his chest.

Dane came around the desk and pressed the barrel into the flesh of Gordov's forehead. Sweat already covered Gordov's tightened face. When the muzzle met skin, he jerked away. Dane pinned his head against the back of the chair.

"Where's the Duchess?"

"I've only seen her once! We communicate through a contact."

"McFadden?"

"Of course! He's the only one who's seen her."

"Why should I believe you?"

"I may be a murderer, but I am not a liar!"

The office door crashed open. Dane jumped behind Gordov. The Russian yelled, "No!"

Dane covered the two new arrivals who stood just inside the office, holding guns in shaking hands. Both were young, one blonde and the other dark haired. The blonde kid Dane did not know, but the other he recognized. The other also had a bruise on his chin.

"This is neat," Dane said to the dark-haired kid. "The bakery wasn't cutting it? Who punched you?"

Fernand Martel, with some spots of flour still on his clothes, blinked rapidly as he held the gun on Dane.

Gordov said, "Put the guns down!"

"You're slipping, Leo. What's with hiring kids? Wait, let me guess. The Duchess put a bunch of angry kids on the payroll. The welfare state ain't working, so now they're giving gangster life a try."

Dane's finger tightened on the trigger. There was no reason he shouldn't put a bullet in the Russian's head, for revenge if nothing else, but Gordov had other crimes to answer for, too.

The Russian said, "Dane, don't—"

Dane let go of the trigger and bashed Gordov on the head once, twice. The Russian slumped forward and his head thumped on the desk. Dane raised the pistol and shot the blonde kid in the shoulder. The kid yelled, dropping his gun, and fell against the door, tumbling to the floor. Dane moved before Fernand fired, the bullet slamming into the wall. Dane stepped close and casually shot Fernand in the right leg, snatching the pistol from the younger man's hands as he fell. Dane kicked the blonde's gun away and regarded the two, one who withered and moaned and the other who curled up and mashed his teeth against the fire in his body.

"Best way to learn is to just dive in," Dane said, and hauled Fernand up against the wall. The dark-haired boy stared at Dane with watery eyes.

"Feel like talking?" Dane said.

Something vibrated in the pocket of Fernand's jeans. Dane tore the pocket off and let a cell phone clatter on the floor. The screen read "Solange".

Fernand blinked.

"Let it go to voicemail and we'll see what she says, huh?"

Chapter Twenty-Four

"When were you planning to tell me you moved?" Dane said.

"Don't start with me, Steve. You vanished on me."

"I'm almost there."

"You don't—"

"Yes, I do. See you in a minute. Oh, a friend is coming by. Inspector Ambard. Make sure you let him in."

"Is he bringing wine?"

"No, just more cops."

"Oh, fun."

Dane let the tubby valet at the Hotel Brittany find a place to park the Porsche. A couple of police cars sat in the loading zone. A short elevator ride brought him to the tenth floor, where he didn't knock on the door to Suite 1006. He turned the knob and smiled at the first person he saw.

Inspector Jean-Louis Ambard.

"Good evening, Inspector."

"Hello," Ambard said. He had two uniformed officers with him. "Now maybe you can explain this…whatever."

Daudet, Alexis, Nina and Solange sat in the middle of

the room. Nina and Solange sat close together. Dane surveyed his audience and, hands clasped behind his back, began a slow stroll around the room. "I suppose you're wondering why I gathered you here today."

Nina said, "Oh get on with it."

"It started a few months ago when a young woman met a young man who worked at a bakery. He seemed nice enough, but he ran with some rough characters, and when he learned more about the young woman's father, he started getting ideas. The girl's father ran a cosmetics company that shipped all over the world and was so well known that his products breezed through customs. The baker decided that sort of thing could help some guys he knew, so they started talking about his ideas and pretty soon more ideas started happening."

Alexis jumped in. "The point is what, Dane?"

"And ruin the suspense? Patience, Alexis. This is too much fun. So, these guys had the idea to use Daudet's shipments to mask a gun-running side operation. They worked for somebody who calls herself the Duchess; problem was, they needed an inside man. That's where you, Alexis, entered the picture."

"That's crazy!" Alexis said, rising.

"Sit down," Inspector Ambard told him.

"Almost done," Dane said. "They put things in motion, but Gerard got in the way. He went to the cops but was too afraid to talk. Y'all are fixin' to move crates of guns out of a certain warehouse, weapons stolen from US arsenals. The Duchess needs money after the failure in Italy. Enter an assassin hired by the Duchess. But not to kill Gerard. The plan was to put him in the hospital and keep everybody else on edge and under cover and not paying attention, hence the death threats—"

"And the stuff at the house," Nina said.

"—while the guns were shipped. Eventually, though, Gerard and Mr. Daudet would have to be taken out."

Ambard said, "How can you prove this, Dane?"

"I'll take you to the warehouse and show you the guns and a bunch of goons who are currently tied up and unconscious. Including a Russian named Gordov. You'll like that catch, Inspector. I'll tell you where to send the reward. Both amounts, by the way. Don't skimp on me."

Inspector Ambard said to Alexis, "Stand up." He took out a pair of handcuffs.

Alexis Daudet stood up. And took out a pistol.

Solange screamed as Alexis raised the gun. The uniformed officers tackled him, one knocking the gun away. They kept Alexis pinned and turned him over so Ambard could lock the cuffs on him.

Nicolas Daudet, standing, watched the policemen lift his son from the carpet. Alexis did not look at his father as Ambard steered him for the door.

Dane said, "I'll see you in thirty minutes, Inspector."

Ambard answered with a wave and went out with his suspect.

Solange sobbed into Nina's shoulder. Dane watched Daudet. The older man stared at the open door the policemen had taken his son through; when he turned to face Dane, he said, "Now what, Mr. Dane?"

The pain etched on Daudet's face made Dane pause. A quick comeback wasn't appropriate, and Dane had to admit that was the first thing to come to mind. Instead he gave the man the truth.

"I don't know, Mr. Daudet. Aftermaths aren't really my area of expertise."

The server brought Dane's tea and Nina's coffee. Nina stirred in cream and sugar, while Dane took a sip right away.

"I was afraid," she said, "you were going to accuse Solange, too."

"The only thing she's guilty of is picking the wrong boyfriend. Won't be the last time, I bet."

"I like that kid."

"Remind you of anybody?"

"Maybe a little. What's next?"

"We're going to Mexico."

"Really? What's in Mexico besides a lot of wonderful tequila for me and Te-Amo cigars for you?"

"That's where the guns were being shipped. We're going to find out who's on the receiving end. Somehow, the buyer knew how to contact the Duchess, and we're going to use that to our advantage. I have a connection there, an army general named Juan Parra. He can help us."

"What about Gordov?"

"We will get the reward for capturing him. That's nothing to sneeze at. It'll keep you in vitamins for ten years."

"I like vitamins," she said. "But doesn't he know anything?"

"He only deals with McFadden."

"What if the person in Mexico only deals with McFadden too?"

"Then I'll see Sean one more time after all," Dane said.

Part III:
The Zeta Connection

Brian Drake

Chapter Twenty-Five

Nuevo Laredo, Mexico

As the jet approached the runway, Dane looked out the window at the US. The Quetzalcoatl International Airport sat near the US–Mexican border, in fact in Nuevo Laredo, sister city of Laredo, Texas. Dane was looking into Texas, but not seeing Texas. Instead he saw the land he'd left behind.

The wheels touched ground and the plane jolted. The roar of the air brakes filled the cabin.

Nina squeezed his right hand. He turned to look at her.

"Where'd you go?"

"I'm right here," he said.

But he hadn't been, really. His reverie wasn't only inspired by a glance in the direction of the United States. A lot more weighed on his mind.

Dane and Nina had been in Paris, preparing for Mexico, when Dane's cell rang. The caller ID read TODD MCCONN. McConn and Dane went back to the days of the 30-30 Battalion. McConn had, at first, been just another operator in Dane's mercenary outfit; eventually they became close friends. Now that the 30-30 days were over, McConn still took odd jobs: security, surveillance, rescue and recovery. Sometimes he worked alone, sometimes with helpers.

Dane answered and greeted his friend. "What's new?"

"It's bad, Steve. General Parra is dead."

Dane felt his legs giving out. He dropped onto the hotel bed, Nina staring at him in concern. He held up a hand to wave her off. She sat next to him with her hands in her lap.

"What happened?"

"One of the cartels took him out. You know the Mexican government has nearly stopped fighting the drug thugs, right?"

"I've read a little about it."

"Parra and as many soldiers as he could muster have been fighting on their own, sort of an outlaw unit, if you will. I was hired to help out with logistics and intelligence. He wanted you here, too."

"I've been busy."

"I'm sure. Anyway, he died last night. He went home with one of his girlfriends, and they got him, Steve. Right through the window."

Dane sat quietly for a moment. He felt hollow. General Juan Parra had been more than a client. He had become one of Dane's most trusted allies.

"We were coming to Mexico anyway, Todd."

"For what?"

Dane explained.

"There might be a connection," McConn said.

"I'm betting there is," Dane said.

"How soon can you get here?"

"Blink once and we'll be getting off a plane."

They found Todd McConn in the baggage claim area holding up a sign that read Major Pane and Dane laughed despite the heavy weight he felt. It was an old joke. The members of Dane's 30-30 Battalion had bestowed the nickname on him for no other reason than that was what soldiers did. It helped that Dane had been a major in the Marines.

"Steve," McConn said, lowering the sign and shaking hands with his old friend. McConn was decked out in black T-shirt, jeans, and black cowboy boots. His usual outfit.

"Nice to see you again, too, Nina."

She smiled at him.

They collected their bags. Nobody said anything. Dane did not want to talk. He specifically did not want to verbally acknowledge General Parra's murder. He pressed his lips together and made his mouth a flat line.

The trio left the terminal and Dane bought a newspaper from a sidewalk vendor. He grimaced at the heat. He felt squeezed by it, as if in a pressure cooker—and that, after only a few seconds. *Welcome to Nuevo Laredo.* He tucked the paper under his right arm.

McConn slid behind the wheel while Dane and Nina sat in back. Dane glanced at the headlines and saw an article about the general. He placed the paper face down on his lap and looked out the window instead.

"He never doubted you'd come if he called," McConn said.

"I guess we've avoided talking about this long enough."

McConn passed him a Te-Amo cigar, lighting his own. They contributed to the smoky haze already filling the bar. It wasn't a large bar, more of a hole in the wall wedged between a laundry and a dance studio. The only light came from the two windows at the front and calling them windows was generous. They were more like the portholes on a cruise ship. The rest of the bar glowed from neon signs advertising this or that and a large-screen television playing an outrageous game show on which the host wore a glittering blue jumpsuit and his taller female companion spilled out of her top.

The bar's air conditioning worked and provided a respite from the blowtorch outside; drinkers escaping the dry heat filled stools and the other tables.

McConn gave Dane and Nina the rundown on his visit and what he'd been doing for General Parra so far. He touched on the assassination but provided no details.

"Where are Parra's people now?" Dane said.

"They're hiding," McConn said.

"I'll need to see them eventually," Dane said. "Who's taking the general's place?"

"A pair named Carlos and Eva. They're married but I have no idea if they're using real names. The whole unit is almost in a state of panic. Parra was killed at his safe house. Nobody but key people knew about the house, Steve."

Nina said, "Somebody's a rat," and downed the remaining tequila in her glass. She reached for the bottle their waitress had kindly left and poured a refill.

Dane puffed on the Te-Amo. He would have preferred one of his Glandon Family cigars, but when in Mexico, he smoked what the locals smoked. It was only polite. Mexico took pride in its cigars, which didn't receive the respect and attention of the Central American blends; Dane did not want to offend his hosts. He said, "So how many knew?"

"Besides Carlos and Eva? Me. It wasn't common knowledge among the team."

"Parra always had a lady friend," Dane said. "Did his current squeeze know about the house?"

"I'll find out," McConn said. "He didn't mention anybody to me."

"No bragging?"

"There have been more important things on his mind. The Mexican government is trying to keep the cartels from shooting up the country, and he thought cutting back on enforcement and prosecutions might help, but the cartel has only grown more violent."

"Shocker."

"I was going over some intel I'd picked up with him the day before he was killed," McConn said. "The enemy is growing in number. Not even Parra and his troops can make a dent. It's as if everything he worked toward his whole life, protecting Mexican citizens from criminals, was going to fail."

"What about other attempts on his life?"

"He didn't say. He wanted me and you and as many men and equipment as we could gather. He wanted us to help change the tide. And that's all we talked about."

"You still have your pictures from the recon you made before he was killed?" Dane said.

"Parra had the originals."

"Who has the originals now?"

"They're gone."

"Of course." Dane drank some beer.

"We need to get going," McConn said. "The general would not be happy if we were late."

Chapter Twenty-Six

At least, Dane decided, we hadn't missed the funeral.

Mexico buried General Juan Parra with full military honors and made no mention of his alleged outlaw status. But Dane could not help but notice that only the required amount of regular army representatives had shown up. If members of Parra's team were present, they did not reveal themselves.

The twenty-one-gun salute broke Dane from his reflection, and the service came to a close. The mourners stood up. Dane watched the honor guard close Parra's casket. The coffin closed with a solid thud, forever sealing its occupant inside. He didn't want his last memory of the general to be the still and serene face in the coffin, but one had to deal with no complaint with what life handed out. Nina tugged on his arm. He faced her and she hugged him.

"I'm sorry, hon."

He squeezed her back.

Presently some of the crowd gathered in clusters for quiet talk, while others made for the cemetery parking lot.

Dane, Nina and McConn stood together watching. Dane felt the temperature rising by the moment and wanted to get out of his black suit as soon as possible.

One couple stood out from the rest, both wiry thin. The male had close-cropped hair and wore a black suit with boots not yet marred by the green grass. The female, who had an arm through one of his, wore a black dress with a hat and veil. Her hair was too short, and her calves too toned for an ordinary Jane, but as they passed by, they did not acknowledge McConn nor he them.

Dane said, "When can I meet Parra's people?"

"First thing tomorrow morning. Eight a.m. sharp."

Nina said, "Good. I like an early breakfast."

McConn dropped them off at their hotel. On the way in Dane told Nina he wanted only a regular room. He didn't feel like indulging in their usual opulence. They unpacked. Dane turned on the A/C and let the cool air blast through. Nina went into the bathroom. Dane sat down by the closed window and read the newspaper. There was indeed no lack of stories regarding the drug war playing out on the streets of Nuevo Laredo, the very streets below.

Gunmen from the Zeta Cartel, the primary player in the area, had ambushed and killed a recently appointed police chief as he'd left his home three days ago, calling it retaliation for a military raid along the Rio Grande in which a cartel commander had been killed.

The murder tally also included a male and female, both in their twenties, who had been hung from each of the international bridges linking the city with the Texas border. The pair had been killed elsewhere first. They had been crusaders, the newspaper said, against the drug cartel, using social media to attack the drug runners and criticize the government for not doing enough to clean up the streets. They were not cops or government agents. The cartel didn't care.

Dane set the newspaper down and let out a breath. He knew all he needed to know about the town now. It wasn't the first war zone he'd ever visited. It wouldn't be the last.

Next morning. Eva Avila, the woman Dane had noticed at the funeral, sleepily rolled over and felt for Carlos, but his side of the bed was empty. The rumpled sheets where he had lain weren't warm; he'd been up for a while. She listened but did not hear him moving about the house. The radio and television were also silent. She bolted up with a pounding heartbeat. Swinging out of bed, she threw on an old robe and went down the hall. He wasn't in the den or kitchen. She called his name, but he did not answer. And then she smelled smoke. She found him in their unfinished backyard, standing near a pile of bricks, smoking a cigarette.

She went over and hugged him from behind. The morning chill brushed her ankles and ran up the hem of the robe. He stood in the shade of the house so the blast from the rising sun did not reach them. "You scared me," she said.

"Did I keep you awake last night?"

"No."

"I couldn't sleep. Must have gotten up ten times."

"I heard the phone ring this morning," she said.

"It was Hector," Carlos said. "There are more Zetas in town than usual. They're looking for us. The only reason I think they didn't attack the funeral was because so few of us were there."

"How many Zetas?"

"Two truckloads, at least. You know there will be more. They came in overnight."

"We aren't going to make it, are we?"

"Hush."

"Will the Americans really be helpful?"

"General Parra told me all about them," Carlos said. "If he believed in them, so can we." He flicked the cigarette away. "We're going to be late if we don't get going."

They took turns showering and jumped into light-colored street clothes. Carlos merged their battered Jeep into traffic, and hot air raced into the open-topped vehicle. After a few minutes of driving, he told Eva to get a 9mm automatic from the glove box.

"What's wrong?" She took out the SIG-Sauer and snapped back the slide.

"Car behind us. It's weaving through lanes."

She looked back. A white Ford missing its front bumper. Two men in front. Windows down. Carlos took the pistol from Eva and tucked it under his right leg. Eva reached under the seat and hauled up a battered MAC-10 with so many scratches and scuffs, it appeared useless; it wasn't. She worked the bolt and held the submachine gun on her lap and wiped sweat from her brow. She could already feel her T-shirt sticking to her back.

Carlos downshifted and sped up. He swung around a pickup full of hay bales. Eva watched the Ford leap ahead to keep up.

Carlos swung right, tires screeching, the Jeep's body leaning left, and stayed at speed through the block of shops and street vendors. The Ford fell behind a little but remained in sight. Carlos made the next sharp left and turned into the parking lot of an empty, boarded-up school.

Eva smiled as they sped between buildings and reached the blacktop of the open playground. The two had planned for an event like this and had previously noted this location as a great place to stand and fight. As

Carlos stomped the brakes, Eva jumped out and ran for a narrow gap between two buildings. She squeezed into the gap and dropped to one knee, brushing away a spider web that tickled the back of her neck. Two Zeta foot soldiers wouldn't swing the tide, she thought, but it was a great way to begin evening the score.

Carlos, kneeling by the front of the Jeep, held the SIG-Sauer in both hands.

The Ford swerved into the lot and stopped near the Jeep. The two men jumped out holding automatic weapons. Carlos fired three times before the two were completely out of the car; Eva triggered a salvo from the MAC-10. The thugs never fired a shot. Carlos hit the driver in the chest and neck. Eva's rounds stitched the other gunman up the center of his back.

The crackling echo of gunfire hadn't faded before Carlos jumped back into the Jeep. "Come on!" he shouted, Eva leaping up beside him. Eva took out her cell phone and started dialing from memory—she had no stored numbers in that particular phone. She began spreading the word. The Zetas weren't stopping with the assassination of General Parra; they were coming after all of them. She hoped her friends would be as lucky as they had been, but also knew that even the best and most skilled warriors eventually fell. Just like she would someday. And Carlos, too.

Chapter Twenty-Seven

Steve Dane did not like the idea of waiting, but also had to admit that his body wasn't quite ready for full throttle. As he stood in the shower, leaning against the wall, not moving, he let the hot water sting his body and kick the overnight soreness away. Getting out of bed had been a serious effort, with every joint stiff and complaining about the movement. He wasn't a young man anymore. His rough-and-tumble lifestyle didn't shake off like it once had.

He emerged from the shower drying his hair. Nina leaned against the dresser, drinking a bottle of water. She smiled as she brushed by and shut the bathroom door and started her own shower. Dane drank the rest of her water and dressed. He was already sweating by the time he finished buttoning his shirt. He turned up the A/C.

Nina came out. "You'll roast in those long sleeves."

"I'll take the risk," he said.

They met McConn at the Nuevo Laredo Café and split a large taquito chilaquiles scramble, consisting of eggs, peppers and onions, with refried beans and hash browns; a second plate of Mexican sausage, rice, and frijoles y tortillas sat next to the first. They forked portions from the larger plates onto their smaller ones.

Nina spread hot salsa over her eggs, a combination Dane did not find appealing until she convinced him to try a taste. The buttery eggs went very well with the salsa, and he mixed some into his own eggs.

"Where are they?" Nina said, speaking over the motors of strategically placed fans that tried to cool the cafe. "They're twenty minutes late."

McConn checked his phone; then, the café door swung open and Carlos and Eva, still flushed from the fight, entered. They joined the trio at the table. McConn made the formal introductions, but they all remained subtle in their greetings and nobody shook hands. Dane offered Carlos and Eva some breakfast, and the pair eagerly dug in.

Carlos explained the delay.

"Was anybody else hit?" McConn said.

"Some of our people haven't answered their phones," Carlos said. "I don't know if that means they were hit or not."

"Nice of them to oblige us this way," Nina said. "Who are the shooters?"

"The drug cartel's army," Dane said. "But they didn't start that way."

McConn jumped in. "They started as a paramilitary force for the government who could meet the cartel head-on."

"What went wrong?" Nina said.

"After we organized the first two battalions," McConn said, "they went to work for the cartel instead."

"Really?"

"Another shining spot for US foreign policy," Dane said.

Carlos said, "What do you mean, *we*?"

McConn said, "I was part of the joint task force of US Special Ops units that came here to train the Zetas."

"You know how they think," Eva said.

"Won't help much," Dane said. "I'm sure they've modified the tactics the US taught them. But I would like to show them that they can't kick sand in our faces like that."

Eva said, "You'll never get them all."

"It's not about that, honey," Nina said.

Dane smiled at Eva.

Carlos said, "The Zetas have a centralized base of operations now. One man controls the force. He houses, trains and supplies weapons."

"Pablo Oliva," McConn said. "Cuban. He went to the cartels and sold them the idea of running their army, so they didn't have to spend their resources."

"Let me guess," Dane said, "that Oliva buys his weapons from somebody called the Duchess."

"How did you know?" Eva said.

"We would have shown up even if General Parra hadn't been killed," Dane said. "I was hoping to enlist his help. Nina and I have been on that woman's trail from Italy to Paris to now."

"She's slippery," Nina said.

"We found a shipment of guns in Paris that was scheduled to arrive here in a few days," Dane said. "It's safe to assume Oliva was expecting them. What new intel were you gathering that may have made them kill the general?"

"Smuggling routes," McConn said.

Carlos continued, "We've been identifying not just the Zetas' growing numbers but the routes they use for both drug and human trafficking."

"The plan," Eva said, "was to hit each route at the same time and close them down."

"And they took the general's files on this," Dane said. "They knew where to go and what to steal. Who was the general's latest girlfriend?"

"Her name is Rosita," Carlos said.

"Was she present the night he was killed?"

"No."

"Of course not. Bring her somewhere safe where we can talk."

"We'll arrange it."

"Where can we get a look at Oliva?"

"That's easy," Carlos said. "He visits a nightclub downtown every night. His daughter sings there."

Dane and Nina stood near the edge of the Rio Grande dividing Nuevo Laredo from Texas. Off to their right spanned one of the two international bridges linking the town to the United States. The second bridge was off to the left. The right-side bridge was full of cars crossing the border, the other bridge had lanes of nothing going nowhere. Dane assumed the cars going to Texas would eventually return via the other bridge.

"We can throw rocks into Texas," Nina said.

"The US might take it as an act of war and invade," Dane said, adding: "That might help, actually."

Dane turned his back to the US side and set his gaze on the Mexican town. It could have been any town in the world. Homes, shops, people living and working and dreaming—or trying to amidst the war raging around them that had claimed so many lives. Places like this were all over the world, and the governing powers, for all their talk, had no power at all over the aggressor forces, due to either incompetence, corruption or apathy. What was one tiny town on a planet of millions of towns? Who cared what happened here?

Just another war zone, yeah. Deep down he knew even his minuscule effort would not turn the tide; still, he could not stand by and let the suffering continue without letting the aggressors know that there was somebody in the world who could not be bought off and had no problems using the same violent tactics as they.

"What are you thinking?"

Dane cracked half a smile. "Same old thing," he said.

"Come on." She pulled on his arm. "I want a beer."

"They call it cerveza here, baby."

"Shut up and drive."

Chapter Twenty-Eight

They found a cantina called Hector's, where they sat at the bar, each with an ice-cold bottle of Carta Blanca.

Customers drifted in and out, either drinking or ordering food. Everybody seemed to be living their lives as best as they could, but their cautious glances betrayed the underlying fear that permeated the town.

Hector, the owner, looked about a thousand years old, with a full head of gray hair and fiery dark eyes.

As Dane and Nina drank, he railed against the "invasion" of cartel soldiers. The murders in the streets, decapitations, the horrors of a drug war they didn't want but that had been visited upon the ordinary citizens anyway.

Dane and Nina listened without comment. There wasn't much they could say. But it wasn't the first time in Dane's experience that innocent people had been dragged into a conflict they did not want; how they reacted and fought back against the injustice, though, separated the sheep from the wolves. So far, the only wolves he'd found willing to fight back were General Parra's people.

Then Hector said, "Why are the two of you here?"

Dane and Nina exchanged looks, but before they could provide an answer, the door dinged open and two big men entered. Chairs scraped the floor and a woman gasped, but nobody moved.

Hector shouted at them to go away.

One of the goons reached across the bar, grabbed a fistful of Hector's apron and smacked him. The other vaulted over the bar. He grabbed a bottle of rum. Dane took out his .45. The goon turned back around and froze.

"Put it back."

The thug grimaced and raised the bottle. Dane shot him in the head. The thug fell back against a shelf of bottles, the shelf collapsing. A shower of bottles landed on his head. Not all of them broke.

Dane swung around to the other, who shoved Hector away and dug for an automatic on his hip. Dane shot him. The thug knocked over a table on his way to the floor.

Hector, leaning on the bar, holding the side of his face with his free hand, stared wide-eyed at Dane. He wasn't the only one. Every customer in the bar locked their eyes on the American and his companion.

Dane put away the .45, swallowed the last of his beer, and put down the bottle. "Sorry about the mess."

Nina then smiled at Hector. "Does that answer your question?" she said.

They made it back to the hotel without further incident, but the swarm of armed Zeta troops, all riding in the backs of Jeeps and pickups, kept them on guard.

"Got a little trigger-happy back there," Nina said.

"What would you have done? This is an occupied town, and it might as well be invisible."

"You've never let things get to you before. Why now?"

"They killed my friend."

"You have a lot of friends. Some are alive and some are dead. What's so special about General Parra?"

Dane said nothing. He poured a drink and lit a cigar and sat at the table. Nina, not pouring a drink of her own this time, sat on the edge of the next chair and leaned close.

"Please tell me," she said.

"There's a reason he wanted me here," he said. "We had the soldier's bond more than anybody I've served with. He hired me for a job, but we got really close—played poker and talked and smoked and drank whiskey into all hours. One night I really screwed up. We were in the middle of a fight, and I almost got shot in the back. I thought the fight was over and stood up. Parra saved my life. After the job was over, I told him if he ever needed me again to call and I'd drop everything and come here. But we were stuck in Paris."

Dane blew out a stream of cigar smoke.

"You didn't fail him. If he wanted to spend the night with his girlfriend, you couldn't have stopped that, either."

"And if she set him up, I'll feed her to a shark," he said.

"I'll bring the rope to tie her up. But where will you get the shark?"

"Same place you got the rope."

It was a quiet cantina, bright neon and low lighting. The stage, currently empty, was the center of attention. Dane and Nina leaned against the bar sipping cervezas. Carlos and Eva, not wanting to show themselves any more than they had to, had withdrawn after the breakfast meeting. Dane had no idea where they had gone, but he knew what they were doing: checking in with the other members of the team. He hoped they all were faring as well as Carlos and Eva against the invading Zeta forces.

A young woman in a tight black dress, her long hair straight down her back, stepped onto the stage to quiet applause. The band picked up their instruments and started playing. Her name was Consuegra Oliva and her father, Pablo, sat in a back-corner booth with a guard on either side. He sat and drank beer and worked on a plate of fajitas. He stopped to applaud with the rest of the crowd.

Consuegra Oliva opened with a jazzy number that brought the place to life. She moved back and forth across the stage, making eye contact with the audience. Dane glanced over at her beaming father. She gave him a finger wave, and he saluted with the bottle.

Nina finished her beer and called for another; as she twisted off the cap, Dane's cell phone vibrated. He went outside and answered.

"Yes?"

McConn said, "The girl's with me."

"Were you able to make the other arrangements we talked about?"

"No trouble. Her phone was easy to tap. Carlos and Eva are going to meet us, too."

"What's their situation?"

"They weren't the only ones hit, but everybody's in one piece and they're all going underground until further notice."

"Okay. We're on our way."

"Get enough of a look at Oliva?"

"He's a proud papa."

"And a murderer."

"True. But his kid likes him."

"Funny how that works, isn't it?"

Chapter Twenty-Nine

"No! Get out!" Hector the bartender came around the bar waving a finger. "Get out!"

Carlos stepped between Dane and the older man. They exchanged words in rapid Spanish, with Hector making accusing gestures at Dane.

Carlos turned to Dane. "You shot two Zetas here?"

"Yes."

"You brought the heat, Dane. Hector's afraid they'll retaliate. He isn't a soldier, but he ferries information through the network. You picked a lousy place for a gunfight."

"Where else can we go?"

Before Carlos could say, Hector exploded with a further salvo of rapid vocabulary; the exchange took several more minutes. Hector's cheeks flared, but he finally threw up his hands and returned to the bar.

"Ten minutes, no more," Carlos said.

A trap door in the back room revealed a flight of stairs. Dane let everybody else go first: Carlos, Eva, Nina and then McConn and Parra's girlfriend, Rosita. She didn't look at him but stayed close to McConn.

Carlos and Eva pulled strings on overhead lights and lit the small room. Bare wood walls, two cots and a table.

"Sort of a last-resort hideout," Carlos explained.

McConn showed Rosita to the table, and she sat down. "Why are you treating me like I did something wrong?" she said, glancing at them all. She hugged her purse close and hunched her shoulders, turned puppy eyes at Dane.

"What happened the night the general died?" Dane said.

She started to cry. It took a few moments for her to speak. "It was a normal night." She sniffed. "We had dinner and were sitting on the couch."

"They shot him through the window."

Rosita moved her head up and down, wiping her eyes.

"Why did he sit on the couch near the window, Rosita?"

"We always did! He wasn't concerned with being killed. We never talked about work. When he was with me, he relaxed. It was the only time he really relaxed."

"Uh-huh."

"You think I did this?"

"I think you set him up."

"Why would I? I've been with him for two years. If I wanted to hurt him, I could have done it sooner. I didn't tell!" She sobbed into her purse.

Dane turned to McConn. "Get her out of here."

McConn helped the woman from the chair. They went up the stairs to the bar and out to the street. McConn put her in the passenger seat of his car and drove off after a cryptic glance at Dane.

Carlos and Eva climbed into their Jeep. Carlos said to Dane, "Do you really think she was involved?"

"That's why we bugged her phone. If she did and knows we know, she'll have to report."

Carlos started the motor. "We're still assuming Oliva is

guilty. What if it was somebody else?"

"Who might that be, Carlos?"

The other man shook his head.

"We'll know soon enough," Dane told him.

Eva waved good-bye as Carlos stepped on the gas.

Rosita sobbed quietly as McConn drove. He wondered if maybe Dane had figured wrong. If she was guilty, she was one hell of an actress.

They didn't talk during the drive, and McConn escorted her up three flights of steps to her apartment, where she entered without saying good-bye. He waited until the deadbolt slammed into place and then returned to his car.

Opening the glove compartment, he took out a black box with an earphone attached. He put the earphone in his left ear and turned on the box. He didn't have to wait long. The sound of Rosita's dialing a telephone came through loud and clear. Ringing began. Another party picked up and a male voice said:

"Yes?"

"It's me. They know everything!"

"We know."

"What?"

"It was only a matter of time."

"What do I do now?"

"You can do whatever you want."

"What? You make me spy for two years and now you cut me loose?"

The line clicked. She screamed and slammed her receiver down.

McConn yanked the earphone and called Dane's cell.

Dane said, "Any news?"

"You were right. First thing she did was call."

"I'll be in touch."

"Don't do anything without me, Steve. Steve?"

Dane had already hung up.

Dane tapped the door with the snout of the .45.

The door opened about an inch. Dane kicked. Rosita yelped as the door smacked her in the face; she fell back, Dane rushing in with Nina behind him. She shut the door. Rosita's nose was bleeding down her upper lip. She spat blood on the carpet. Dane grabbed her hair and pulled. She screamed, forcing herself up; Dane flung her onto the couch. He leaned close and put the .45 against her head.

"What did you tell them?" he said to Rosita.

"I didn't—"

Dane jabbed her in the throat with the .45. She gagged. "We tapped your phone, honey. We know everything, remember?"

"I told them about Juan's house!" she said.

"For how much?"

"Twenty thousand US," she said.

"What, no sick mother who needs an operation?"

"You're going to kill me anyway!"

Dane's finger tightened on the trigger.

"She's not worth it," Nina said. "Don't waste the bullet."

Dane relaxed and stepped back. "Maybe."

"She's useless to them now. Did they already pay you?"

Rosita jerked her head up and down.

"I suggest you get out of town fast," Nina said. "You've probably been here too long already."

Dane put away his gun and went to the door. He went out, leaving the door open. Nina followed, but stopped long enough to turn and wink.

Dane said to Carlos, "Time to gather the troops," and outlined his plan.

"Are you sure a direct assault is a good idea?" Carlos said.

"Once Oliva is out of the way, his people will be too concerned with the power vacuum to worry about us. What we need from him is information on the Duchess, and then we can cut off the supply of guns for good."

"They'll find another."

"And we'll come back and kill that person too."

"Okay," Carlos said. "I'll send you the coordinates to the camp."

Dane hung up and called McConn and told him to stand by. He grinned at Nina. "Now the real fun begins," he said. "Time for some payback."

Chapter Thirty

Dane slowed the truck as it bumped along, the road full of ruts and rocks. "Should be right around this corner," he said.

Nina sat beside him, with McConn in the back with their gear. The dry mountain country was about as far from anywhere as they could get and probably the best place to assemble an armed force, though Dane knew from his own experience that such camps were best in place for only a short time.

Dane steered the truck around the corner and slowed to squeeze between two boulders on either side of the pass. Two men in camouflage holding automatic weapons stepped into view. Dane stopped the truck. He and Nina and McConn raised their hands. One of the soldiers came up to Dane's window, looked at him a moment, and said, "Follow us," in accented English.

The troops started moving, and Dane eased the truck along behind them. Presently they entered a clearing surrounded by low hills; the camp was a tent city, with large and small tents set up in rows, large trucks and Jeeps the only vehicles. Troops were spaced out along the outer perimeter in foxholes, each with a heavy machine gun. Others milled about the camp.

The two escorts stopped at one of the larger tents where Carlos stood waiting. He was dressed for battle in green fatigues, a pistol on his right hip and a rifle across his back. His shirt stuck to his body. A bandana tied around his forehead was soaked through; Dane looked around and saw that pretty much every soldier had a bandana around his or her forehead and felt the wetness on his own. He did not have a bandana. When he stepped out of the air-conditioned truck, he decided he'd better scrounge up a few for him, Nina and Todd.

"Welcome to Valle de Zorro, the Fox Valley," Carlos said.

"This would otherwise be a nice place," Dane said.

"It is a nice place," Carlos said, leading the trio inside.

A map lay across a table in the center of the room. No chairs. Glossy photos were pinned on the canvas walls. Large battery-powered fans circulated the air, and rocks weighed down the corners of the map. The pinned-up pictures flapped in the machine-generated breeze.

Eva, in fatigues of her own but carrying only a holstered pistol, stood near the table with her lips a flat line. She only nodded at the new arrivals; the other soldiers in the room listened to Carlos's introduction, and then he directed the three to the map on the table.

"This is Oliva's estate," he said, speaking over the noise of the fans. "House in the center of the property, walls all around, hills in the back. He has about twenty troopers there."

"That's all?" Nina said. "What about reinforcements?"

"There is a barracks ten miles east, accessible by a two-lane road."

"I see the plan already," McConn said.

"I have men ready to hit the barracks," Carlos said. "The rest of the force—"

Explosions rocked the compound, and a line of automatic weapons fire stitched a jagged line in the wall behind Eva. Heavy machine gun fire hammered back in response. Everybody hit the floor. Carlos and Dane crawled to the door and looked out. Two pit gunners and a trooper firing from a Jeep sprayed bursts at a large group of armed men rushing toward the camp across open ground. Men yelled, ran to positions; more machine gun fire crackled throughout the camp.

The radio attached to Carlos's web gear sparked to life. *"Zeta forces attacking!"*

Carlos radioed back. "All troops, do whatever you have to do to repel!"

More slugs tore through the tent walls; more explosions echoed. Dane and Carlos raced outside. Nina and McConn followed Dane while the soldiers went with Eva, who was shouting orders.

The Jeep ahead took fire, the gunner's head snapping back. Dane leapt for the gun as the soldier fell. He turned the muzzle on the approaching force and yanked back the trigger. Flame spat from the barrel of the big American M-60, the weapon hammering against his shoulder. He did not aim but instead fired into the attack force. The bright flame from the muzzle made using the sights useless. Some bullets missed but others found a home, and as Nina, McConn, Carlos and the two pit gunners fired their own assault weapons, more of the attackers fell and others sought cover.

The battle raged throughout the camp. Two tents were already on fire, and the flames licked at other, nearby tents;

Carlos's men fought from cover or in the open as the Zetas continued their advance.

Dane's weapon clicked dry. He opened the action and pulled a second belt of ammo from a container near his feet. Bullets split the air, whined off the windshield frame. Dane locked the ammo in place and opened fire again. The Zetas were getting closer. He wiped sweat from his face and eyes.

One of Carlos's men, carrying a flame thrower, ran to the Jeep, stopped near the driver's side and sent an arc of flame toward the Zetas. Some of the men screamed as fire engulfed them. On the ground, brush and bushes caught fire, and soon a screen of searing heat stood between their position and the attacking force.

Over Carlos's radio: *"Helicopters approaching from the east!"*

"Are they ours?"

"No way to tell—here they come!"

Three helicopters hopped over the eastern rise. One broke off and dived low, and door gunners on either side started firing into the camp.

The other two choppers unleashed rocket fire that smashed into the ground with tremendous force.

Dane spotted a cluster of Zeta troopers going for a break in the firewall. He fired, cutting two down and driving the others back.

The choppers zoomed overhead and began to circle back.

Dane dropped into the foxhole beside Carlos. "Where are your helicopters?"

"Hidden in the mountains about five miles south!"

More rockets pounded the camp as the three choppers flew over again; thick, eye-stinging smoke wafted through-out. Eva and another soldier broke through the smoke and reached the foxhole. Eva said, "They've broken through!"

"We need to get to those choppers, Carlos!" Dane said.

"The camp will be embers before we could get back!" Eva said.

"We can't stay here!" Nina said.

Carlos said to Dane, "Can you fly?"

"No," Dane said, "but Todd can."

"He can take one and I'll take another," Carlos said. "Get in the Jeep. Everybody, come on!"

Chapter Thirty-One

One of the helicopters swung away from the camp to follow the Jeep. Dane swung the M-60 around and fired at the approaching craft. Sparks on the undercarriage signaled hits. The chopper flew overhead, the left door gunner leaning out and strafing the ground near the Jeep. The jolting vehicle made a straight bead impossible. Dane fired. The salvo struck the doorway, the gun and the gunner. The gunner pitched forward, falling from the chopper, landing hard on the ground behind the Jeep.

Dane had about six inches left in the ammo belt. As the chopper started to turn away, Dane fired into the cabin and cockpit. The chopper rocked from side to side and then dived into a hillside. The explosion peppered the dirt road with hissing pieces of metal debris.

Carlos, eyes forward, kept driving; Dane locked a third belt into the gun and caught Nina's eye. She was sweaty and dirt clung to her face, and her ponytailed hair was an unruly mess. She was beautiful. She blew him a kiss.

The two UH-1 "Huey" gunship helicopters, similarly armed, sat next to each other in a hollowed-out, open-topped mountain. Carlos swung the Jeep through a short entry tunnel and stopped. The crew piled out. McConn jumped behind the controls of one helicopter and fired up the motor as Carlos did the same with the other.

Dane and Nina joined McConn, each strapping into one of the door guns on either side. These door guns were long-barreled Browning .50-calibers, fully loaded. Other armament included missiles pods. Eva joined Carlos. As the rotors spun, the wind they generated filled the cavern. Carlos lifted off first and rose through the opening. Mc-Conn followed, and the two pilots steered for the columns of rising smoke in the distance.

When they were within range of the camp, the two Zeta choppers turned toward Carlos and McConn, side-mountain guns blazing. Carlos fired a salvo of missiles that blasted one of the Zetas out of the sky. As the flaming black cloud filled the blue sky, the second chopper made a sharp left turn. McConn countered the move, exposing the Zetas to Dane's gunsight. Steve Dane blasted into the backside of the enemy chopper. It swung around to Nina's side and she gave it another burst, and a trail of black smoke poured out the back.

McConn circled behind the smoking chopper while Dane and Nina fired at Zeta targets on the ground. The fight below still raged, with Carlos's troops and the Zetas engaging in close fighting or hand-to-hand combat.

The smoking helicopter swung left again. McConn fired a missile that flashed past the canopy. He corrected with a touch of stick and rudder and fired again. The missile struck dead center. McConn felt the wave of heat from the fireball as he flew by.

McConn turned back for the camp. The battle wasn't over by a long shot.

The battle raged almost five hours. The remains of the tents smoldered, and the echoes of gunfire and explosions still hung in the air, but the Zetas had been driven back. Carlos's people did not bother so much with the buildings as they took care of the wounded and the dead.

Later in the evening, Dane found Carlos sitting alone under a tree smoking a cigarette. He sat next to the other man but said nothing. Carlos, cross-legged, had a thousand-yard stare on his face, his neck and shoulders tight from the burdens on his mind.

"Forty-seven dead and over a hundred wounded," Carlos said. "We can't go on like this." He exhaled a stream of smoke.

"What's the alternative, Carlos?"

"Run. Anywhere."

"And the people looking to you for leadership? What do they do?"

"They run. Anywhere."

"Some people aren't made for running."

"My troops have been slaughtered and my equipment blasted to hell. What's left to fight with? We don't have a treasury. Oliva can buy what he wants from the Duchess, but we have to scrounge and steal and hide. Where do we go?"

"We have enough gas left," Dane said, "for one chopper. I say we load up and take this fight straight to Oliva."

"But—"

"It's the last thing he'll expect," Dane said.

Carlos traced a line in the dirt with one finger.

"Carlos? I'm going with or without you."

"Okay," the other man said. He stubbed out his cigarette in the dirt. "I'd hate for you to get lost."

"Have you seen Nina?"

"I think she's over by the creek."

Dane walked through the camp. Some tended to the wounded, while others loaded every piece of equipment that was still usable onto trucks. The focus and determination on the faces of Carlos's men were no surprise to Dane. Yes, it had been a bad day and many of their comrades were dead, and now they had to withdraw. But the fight would not end today. Tomorrow was another day, as somebody once said, and they would have their revenge.

Dane left the perimeter and followed a worn path to the creek, where he found Nina rinsing off her arms and face. Dane's boots snapped a twig. She reached for her gun.

"Don't shoot."

Nina put down the Smith & Wesson 9mm and sat in the dirt. Dane sat beside her. He tossed a pebble into the water. The water rippled.

She said, "I had to get away from there."

"I don't blame you."

"How's Carlos?"

"He wants to quit. It's hard not to agree with him."

"But you didn't," she said.

"We're going to load up a chopper and go to Oliva's. We'll take the party to him."

"I'll bring a bottle of wine."

"I was thinking something a little more potent."

Dane stood and held out a hand. She grasped it and he pulled her up. She threw her arms around him and squeezed tightly. He closed his eyes and squeezed her back.

"We were supposed to be on vacation, remember?" she

said. "Before all this started."

"Are you getting tired?"

"I think I'd like to slow down for a while," she said.

He let go and she stepped back, but he still held her close. "We always say that and then—"

"You're right," she said. "Can't we put it on hold for a month or so? Or at least until I get bored. That might only take two weeks."

"Anything for you, sweetie."

"And no accordion players to disturb us like in Venice."

"If one shows up, I will crush his skull with my bare hands."

She laughed and broke away. "That would take a miracle," she said. "And this is getting too serious. Let's go."

Dane followed behind her with a grin that quickly faded.

Chapter Thirty-Two

They scrounged fuel, ammo, and leftover rockets from one chopper to fully load the other. Eva rode shotgun, with Carlos at the helm. Dane, Nina, and McConn sat in the back cabin. They lifted off as the crescent moon vanished behind clouds.

It wasn't a long trip. Shortly the flatland where Oliva's mansion sat appeared, and Carlos flipped switches to arm rockets. Troops on the ground saw the chopper and opened fire. Their muzzle flashes winked at Dane and company from the ground, sparks of light in the darkness. Bullets smacked against the chopper as Carlos dove and fired the rockets. Dane and Nina, at the Browning door guns once again, returned fire at targets of opportunity. The rockets struck the house, flames and debris blasting skyward; as Carlos flew over the fire, some of the debris pelted the helicopter.

Dane swung the Browning .50-cal on a cluster of troops on the ground and hosed. The gunners twitched and spun as the slugs cut through them before falling to the ground.

Carlos circled the mansion, Nina strafing the building with machinegun fire. Carlos fired more rockets at ground troops and swung around again for a direct shot at the mansion. More ground fire shook the chopper, and Carlos screamed as bullets hammered through the floor, cutting through his legs and stomach. Eva called his name as Carlos pitched forward, the chopper diving; Carlos raised his body enough to pull back on the stick, but the chopper continued a straight path toward the building.

Carlos shouted, "Jump!" The helicopter drifted close to the ground. Carlos hauled back on the stick. The nose pitched up. "Jump!"

Dane, Nina and McConn grabbed their gear and leapt from the chopper. Eva lunged forward and grabbed Carlos around the neck as the Huey hit the mansion like a brick through a window and the explosion obliterated an entire section of the house.

Flames from the house and fires from the rocket blasts kept the battlefield bright and smoky. There wasn't much resistance. A few troops fired their way, but the trio returned fire as they ran for the house. They split up in the foyer. Dane raced up a curving staircase, squeezing off bursts from his short-barreled FN-FAL at two troops on the upper landing. He jumped over their fallen bodies, scanning for more troops before he advanced. He heard shooting elsewhere in the house but saw no other threat as he stepped through a pair of open double doors and entered a private study. He slung his FAL rifle and headed for the exposed wall safe on the opposite side of the room. It hadn't been opened. Which meant Oliva hadn't made it to study. Had he been killed or injured? Dane opened a pack on his belt and took out a small plastic explosive, which he attached to the safe. He set the digital timer for six seconds and ducked behind a chair. The blast ripped the door off the safe and sent it flying across the room, where it hit the other wall with a thud.

Automatic weapons fire popped some more as Dane stuffed a ledger and a roll of papers under his fatigue blouse. He ran back to the hallway—still clear—and hustled back down the stairs. He continued through the house, linking up again with Nina and McConn, who reported some close shaves while Dane had been playing around upstairs. He suggested they scoot before the men outside devised a plan to come inside, and Nina led the way to a garage, where they climbed into a Hummer and McConn dropped behind the wheel.

McConn started the motor. He crashed through the garage and sped along a concrete path to a closed gate. Dane and Nina fired out the windows at random targets. The steel gate whined and scraped against the Hummer as McConn crashed through. Dane and Nina peered out the back, saw the pursuing pickup and shouted for McConn to step on the gas.

Nina blasted out the back window and Dane tossed a grenade at the pickup. The bomb exploded to one side. Gunfire from the truck punched into the Hummer. Dane lobbed another grenade. It exploded on the road in front of the truck, but the driver swerved, the side of the truck taking most of the blast. Nina fired at the truck's tires. Dane pitched another grenade, his last, but the bomb bounced off the road and exploded in the bushes.

Gunfire from the truck stitched the Hummer, tearing through the back seat but missing Nina and Dane. Dane reloaded his rifle and fired on the truck as Nina lobbed her first grenade, the blast missing.

"Goin' off-road!" McConn shouted, swinging the wheel

left, the Hummer jolting as the tires gouged the ground. Nina tossed a grenade that blew down a tree, blocking the path. The truck crashed into the trunk.

"We aren't going to get very far this way," Dane said, the dust from the dry ground enveloping the Hummer. "Do you have any—"

"All I know is that truck isn't behind us anymore," McConn said.

Nina looked out the back window. "Here comes another chopper!"

The helicopter dived, sending a line of machinegun fire across the front of the Hummer, shredding the hood. The front end pitched forward and dug into the dirt, throwing McConn, Dane and Nina forward; the chopper flashed by overhead and started to turn.

"Out!" Dane shouted, scrambling for a door handle. "Out, out, out!"

The trio ran as the helicopter unloaded another salvo of machinegun fire that split the Hummer in two.

Dane, Nina and McConn sprinted across open ground, heading for a rock formation. Dane looked over his shoulder to see the chopper swooping around again. They reached the rocks and climbed between them. The chopper flew over without firing; McConn tried to take a shot but could not line up his sights fast enough.

"Why didn't they shoot?" Dane said.

"Over there!" Nina said, pointing. Two trucks in the distance stirred up a pair of dust clouds. Coming closer.

The chopper approached again, slowed, and hovered over the rocks.

"This can't be good," Dane said.

The door gunner kept a hot muzzle and his steely eyes on them. The trucks moved closer. When they reached the rocks, the chopper dipped forward and took off the way it had come. Troops piled out of the trucks and ordered them to step away. They did as they were told.

But not before Dane had a moment to jam the ledger and papers in a crevice.

Chapter Thirty-Three

Pablo Oliva checked his watch as the driver steered onto the warehouse property. He didn't want to spend too much time with his captives. He wanted to meet them, to see what all the fuss had been about, and send them to their maker before his daughter's second show of the evening. As soon as he had received word of their capture, he ordered them brought to the warehouse. His last stunt, hanging two troublemakers from the international bridges, had caused such a stir, he wanted these three hung from there too.

The driver braked the car in front of the main door, which was already open. Oliva told him to leave the car running and stepped out. One of his soldiers escorted him inside.

The soldier guided Oliva along the open portion of the warehouse floor to the back office, where two more guards stood. Sitting on the floor were the three captives, their hands untied, but stripped of all weapons. Their pockets had been torn off and every possible hiding place exposed.

Oliva smiled at the man with the close-cropped hair. One of his sleeves had been rolled back, and Oliva noted what looked like burn scars on his arm.

"I had to meet you," Oliva said. "I had to see who it was who inspired General Parra and his people. I admit you are not who I thought you'd be."

"That British guy is on holiday," Dane said.

Oliva only chuckled. "I wasn't even at the mansion, you know," he said. "If 'that British guy' had been here, I'm sure he'd have spent more time gathering proper intelligence."

Dane grimaced.

"It's been a dangerous couple of years down here," Oliva said. "A lot of violence and death. Unnecessary, too. For some reason our society is consumed with the fight against people like me. But only a small portion of society. The rest only want to keep their heads down and survive long enough to see their grandchildren. People like you are a minority, and nobody cares. But you keep fighting as if it's the most important thing in the world."

"You want a response?"

"There are no more heroes in the world or causes worth fighting for," Oliva said. "Why not enjoy your days, indulge yourself? Life is too short to mess with this unpleasantness."

"You're just spinning wheels, pal."

"No, I am making a point. You have sacrificed your life for nothing. Why?"

"I could explain, but you probably wouldn't listen anyway," Dane said. "And if you listened, you probably wouldn't understand."

Oliva chuckled. "I know you wanted to avenge General Parra, and you made a terrific attempt. The game is over," he said. To the troops: "Hang them from one of the bridges like the other two."

Pablo Oliva smiled and marched out.

"Makes you wonder why he bothered," Nina said.

The troopers gestured with their weapons, and the trio stood up.

"I'll see him again," Dane said.

The motorboat chugged along the river with the two international bridges in the distance. At this time of night there were no cars crossing either bridge.

One Zeta soldier steered the boat, while two others sat across from Dane, Nina and McConn. Their hands had been tied, but not behind their backs.

Dane watched the bright lights of Laredo, Texas, on the other side of the border. He had never imagined that the last view he might see would be this side of Texas. He had no intention of dying tonight, but if the end had really come, there were a hundred other sights he would have rather been looking at.

He raised an eyebrow at Todd McConn, who winked back.

He said, "Can you steer this thing, Nina?"

"I can do *anything*, lover," she said.

One of the troops raised his rifle.

"Now!"

Dane and McConn lunged at the troopers, knocking them over the side, splashing into the cold water. Nina clutched her hands together and bashed the driver in the side of the face, shoving him over the side; she turned back to where Dane and McConn were still fighting in the water, splashing and grunting and disturbing the quiet night. The fight did not last long, and soon the pair climbed back into the boat, dripping wet but victorious.

They let forty-eight hours tick by before venturing out again, and when they did leave, they took off in different directions. Dane had two people in town whom he wanted to see. Nina and McConn departed for the rock where Dane had left the information stolen from Oliva's safe.

There was nothing left to do but tie up the loose ends and hit the road. Parra's troops were scattered. Dane had no idea who would replace Carlos and Eva or, worse, how to find them. But he felt confident they would regroup and continue the fight. Someday.

Hector's Café. Dane regarded the place thoughtfully from the other side of the street, puffing on a cigar and watching customers come and go. He watched Hector through the front window as the proprietor wiped his counter and served customers.

Dane finished the Te-Amo and tossed it in the street, crossing during a break in traffic. He entered. The bell above the door dinged; Hector looked up, turned away, and hurried to check each table to ensure that his customers were comfortable.

Steve Dane took a stool at the bar. He traced a fingertip along a crack in the Formica top.

Hector came around, clapped his hands together. "You're back. Just you this time?"

"Hello, Hector."

"You want a cerveza?"

"How about the truth."

"I don't—"

Dane slid off the stool and opened his coat enough to show Hector the .45 hanging under his arm. "Let's go in back a second."

Hector swallowed and stepped around the bar and walked ahead of Dane into the back office. A cluttered metal desk occupied a corner and a matching shelf stood opposite. A pile of empty boxes sat in another corner.

"We had some bad stuff happen, Hector. A lot of our

friends are dead. Carlos and Eva among them."

"I only heard—"

"About the camp, right. Funny thing about that. Carlos told me that you passed messages through the network. You knew about the camp before anybody, yet somebody tipped off the Zetas that we were in those mountains."

"Obviously there was a leak."

"Your place is still standing, Hector. You who were so worried about the Zetas retaliating, yet you are still here. What kind of deal did you make?"

Hector's mouth opened and closed.

Dane took out the .45 and clicked off the safety.

Hector backed up a step.

"You sold us out."

"You don't understand." Back another step.

"Yes, I do."

"I didn't mean—" and he bumped against the wall. He balled his fists. His eyes widened.

Dane raised the gun. Hector winced.

Dane held the gun for a few moments and watched Hector sweat and make little squeaking noises in his throat.

He lowered the gun.

"I'm not going to shoot you, Hector. But you'll wish I had. You get to live with yourself. Or try to."

"The others—they'll kill me!"

"You might never hear them coming."

Dane put away the .45 and turned and walked out. He heard Hector let out a loud exhalation. Dane walked out with his jaw clenched and his stomach tight, but he walked out. Hector, like Rosita earlier, was just another mouse. Not worth a bullet.

But the next name on Dane's list *was* worth a bullet and it was a shame that he would need only one.

Chapter Thirty-Four

That evening Consuegra Oliva finished her set to rousing applause. She blew a kiss at her father, who watched from his booth. She stepped off the stage and went to her dressing room.

Opening the door, she frowned. The light was off. She had left it on. She hit the switch, shutting the door, and then gasped as a man with a gun jumped out of a chair. She tried to fight, but he brushed her blows aside and hit her over the head with the pistol.

Dane grabbed the woman before she collapsed and placed her on a nearby couch. He returned to his chair and sat with the .45 in his lap.

After a few moments, somebody knocked on the door. "Connie?" The doorknob turned and Oliva stuck his head in.

"Come in, Pablo."

Oliva, his eyes on the dark muzzle of Dane's automatic, stepped inside and closed the door.

"Take a seat."

Oliva gave his daughter an anxious glance.

"She'll wake up."

Oliva sat at the dressing table. "I didn't expect you to

come back," he said. "Most people—"

"You misjudged me," Dane said. "Everybody misjudges me. They think I'm just another schnook. And now you get to listen to my speech. You might be right about society being apathetic. In fact, I think you are right. They aren't engaged in anything as noble as raising families. They'd rather watch television and play video games and follow celebrities on Twitter than pay attention to important things like, you know, life and liberty and the law. I get that. Some of us know the world can be better. We won't stop fighting until people like you are gone. Tonight, I'm going to shoot you, because you killed some friends of mine. But not just them. There are plenty of others for whom justice has been long delayed."

"My daughter—"

"She'll get you a nice casket, I'm sure."

"She knows what I do. She'll take over. You won't stop anything."

"Thanks for the tip. I have extra bullets. Might as well not waste the opportunity."

Oliva dashed from the table and Dane shot him. Oliva fell on his face, gagging on blood, thrashing as he tried to crawl the last remaining distance between him and Dane; Dane stood over Oliva and fired again. Oliva stopped thrashing. He lay on the ground with his hands outstretched, mere inches from Dane's ankles.

Dane considered the daughter a moment. She breathed easily, the welt on her forehead growing by the minute. He looked down at Oliva and back to her.

Not this time. Not tonight. She hadn't done anything to hurt anybody—yet. Maybe her father was wrong. Maybe he wasn't. But there was no reason to do anything about her now.

Dane holstered the .45.

Footsteps pounded down the hallway. Dane ran to the window, easing his body through and dropping into the outside alley. He started running. He did not look back.

Dane reunited with Nina and McConn back at the hotel. They had retrieved the ledger and papers from the rock where Dane had stashed them. The items had been unmolested.

It took an hour to go through the material. They had enough information to deliver a death blow to the cartel's operations, information that they could pass along to the remainder of Parra's force once another contact could be located. But there was one piece of information Dane tore from the ledger that he held up for display.

"Here's how we contact the Duchess," Dane said, tapping the piece of paper.

"Where?" Nina said.

"New York City. Let's bring her something she can't refuse," Dane said.

"Like what?" McConn said.

"The latest and greatest in small arms technology currently on its way into the Army inventory."

"You aren't thinking—"

"Yes," Dane said. "Let's get her an M5205."

"Think you can get one?"

"I *know* where I can get one," Dane said. "And I know who can get it for us."

"Anna Dalen?" Nina said.

"Yes."

Part IV:
The Hard Way

Chapter Thirty-Five

The truck had seen better days. Now, not a sliver of cabin glass remained, ditto the tires. Only the bare wheels, pitted with rust, hung on to the wrecked body. Most of the running bits lay scattered around the 1-ton pickup like so many Legos left on a carpet by a child who had run off and would face the wrath of his mother after she sobered up.

"How many people have fired at that truck?"

"Too many," said Anna Dalen. She stood next to him with her hands in the pockets of her leather jacket. She might be an arms dealer, and she might have some questionable clients, but slaying dragons sometimes required one to have questionable friends.

"This is your private shooting range? Aren't you afraid the authorities are going to snoop around?" Dane's gaze swept the green valley. They were deep in the hills, about 20 miles from Anna's home in the south of France.

"I own this land," she said, "and the authorities. Ready to try it out?"

Footsteps crunched the dirt behind him. Dane turned. Dan Hunter, Anna's main squeeze, lifted the M5205 from the trunk of the car. He rested it on his shoulder. The weapon had a large barrel and a cylindrical revolving magazine. The bores of the magazine were at least an inch and a half in diameter and designed to hold high-explosive projectiles. It was the latest in small-arms mass destruction built for the US military, which wanted something troops could carry into urban battlefields. It packed more punch than a rifle or machinegun. Hunter handed the weapon to Dane. It wasn't any heavier than 10 pounds and had a standard pistol grip and trigger combination. Hunter held out a large projectile that resembled a 12-ounce soda pop can but with a rounded tip.

Dane inserted the projectile into the M5205's firing chamber. "What's in the can?"

"High explosive."

"Say good-bye to your truck."

They were 50 yards away from the target, a safe enough distance, Dane figured. He aimed through the top-mounted scope and eased back the trigger. The weapon slammed against his shoulder. The projectile smashed through the driver's door and exploded. The shock of the blast reached them and forced Dane back a few steps.

"That's some power," Dane said.

"In an urban setting, it's downright atomic," Hunter said.

"You're going to take it?" Anna said.

"I'm not only going to take it, I'm going to make a trap out of it," said Dane.

"Be careful baiting that trap," Anna said, as fire consumed the truck and black smoke climbed skyward. "Especially if it's for the Duchess." The metal popped and snapped as the fire ate away at what remained of its guts.

Dane raised an eyebrow. "Will you take a check?"

Dane stayed with Anna and Hunter that night, and they flew him back to Mexico the next day. He arrived late in the afternoon.

Dane steered the rented Jag F-type convertible up the winding road along the coast. The soft leather seats held him in place, and the powerful motor grumbled as the car rocketed along, the tires gripping the road.

He jammed the brakes and swung into the hotel parking lot; the three-building spread at the top of the hill. The bright white stucco stood out like a flame against the rocky mountain behind. He parked the car, stepped out and looked around. The ocean shimmered, the white tips of the waves cascading onto the beach. This resort on the Mexican coast was the exact opposite of Nuevo Laredo, and the irony was not lost on him.

He snapped a salute and a smile at the doorman and crossed the wide and ornate lobby to the elevators, each doorway rimmed with flakes of gold.

He entered the two-room suite and crossed the thick carpet to the deck, where a bikini-clad Nina lay on a lounger soaking up the sun. Her tanned skin glistened. She sipped from a glass of red wine, and a half-empty bottle rested beside the lounger.

"Keeping busy?"

"You didn't tell me you'd be gone overnight."

"Bad cell service."

"Liar. So how did it go? Where's the gun?"

"Anna has it. She'll keep it until we need it."

"You gave her money and didn't bring the gun back?"

"You can't bring something like that back on an airplane, honey."

"Was it a big gun? Does it take lots of bullets?"

"Explosive shells, and yes."

"It makes stuff go boom?"

"Very loudly. I toasted a poor innocent truck."

"Truck killer!"

"Is that your second bottle or your first?"

"First, honey."

"You mean your first today?"

"Do you think I'm a lush?"

"You need to learn how to knit or something."

She held up a hand. "Potty break. Help me up."

He grabbed her hand and half hauled her upright. She weaved a little; he grabbed her sweat-sticky waist and pulled her close.

"Let go," she said, pushing back. "I'll pee all over you."

"You are such a turn-on."

"I know. Let me go."

"That joke writes itself." He gave her a shove through the door and a smack on the bottom.

"Todd will be here in a few minutes," she said.

Dane closed the sliding door and took a sip from the wine bottle, grimaced and put it down. Wine wasn't his thing, but he had plenty of Maker's Mark and Coke. He reopened the sliding door and went to mix a proper drink.

Dane pulled a chair over next to the lounger and lit a cigar. He swallowed some Maker's and Coke and kept a tight grip on the glass. Nina returned, stretched like a cat on the lounger, let out a relaxing sigh.

"Why are you angry with your glass?"

"Huh?"

"The way you're holding it. You're going to break the glass and spill your vitamins all over the deck."

He set down the glass. His hand and fingers were tight. He flexed them a few times.

"Anxious, I guess."

Todd McConn arrived and settled his lanky frame in a lounger, tipped up his feet clad in lizard-skin boots. Dane poured a drink for his old friend.

McConn said, "Do I get to see this supergun?"

"Anna still has it." Dane filled him on the test firing. McConn let out a low whistle.

"How come we never had toys as cool as that?"

Dane shrugged and took another drink.

Nina said, "I'm hungry."

"Always," Dane said.

They had lunch sent up and ate on the deck.

"What's the plan, Steve?" McConn said.

"Simple. We go to New York, meet the Duchess's contact there, and offer to sell the weapon."

"You're crazy."

Dane regarded them both without comment and then looked away.

Nina added, "You want to see the Duchess yourself, right? Go in there with McFadden hanging around and we won't last ten seconds."

"Who's McFadden?" McConn said.

"His first name is Sean," Dane said. "He was part of 30-30 before you joined. Former IRA. Now he's free-lance. We've clashed with him a few times already. I keep trying to get him to come back to the fold, the good side, if you will, but he won't budge."

"Think he'll rat you out?"

"I don't know."

"Let me make the approach," McConn said. "They don't know me."

"McFadden is not going to switch sides," Nina said.

"You'll risk everything if you go in, Steve," McConn

said.

"He thinks his protégé will come to his senses, Todd."

Dane lit another cigar.

Nina said, "Sean has made his choice. If you go through with this—"

"I'm making the approach," Dane said. "Todd, you hang back and cover me. All the way."

"Want me to fly to the moon by waving my arms, too?"

"We leave in two days," Dane said.

"This is insane," Nina said.

Dane didn't budge. "The contact is a man named Alek Savelev."

Nina sat up. "Wait, who?"

"Savelev," Dane said. "He's the US contact for the Duchess."

"This," she said, "just keeps getting better."

"What's the problem now?" McConn said.

"Alek Savelev was my captain when I was in the FSB," she said. "This means I should make the approach." She pointed at Dane. "You can be *my* wingman."

Dane grinned and smoked his cigar. But there was no laughter in his eyes.

Chapter Thirty-Six

New York City

"We're being watched."

Alek Savelev covered his reaction with a sip of latte. The young man who had spoken sat across from him at the small table. In the crowded coffee shop, it was hard to scan all the faces. But his student had seen one, multiple times, and finally, when he was sure, mentioned the man's presence. Savelev swallowed his coffee and said, "Which one, Joe? Dark hair, black suit, thin tie, reading a newspaper?"

Joe frowned. "You know? I thought—"

"I was waiting to see how long you'd take. When did you first see him?"

"About three blocks back."

"Good work. That's about when I saw him. Now, questions."

"Who is he? Who sent him? What does he want, and how long has he been watching?"

"You haven't spotted him before?"

"No. None of the others have reported being followed, either."

Savelev pressed his lips together. "Nobody's been on my tail," he said. "I think we need to see this gentleman up close and personal." He pulled out a cell phone and dialed a number. "It's me," he said. "Who's with you? Grab him and come to the Starbucks on 57th. Call me again when you're a block away. Don't get any closer than that." He hung up and drank more coffee. "Want another?" he said.

"We keep talking?" Joe said.

"He's not a lip reader," Savelev said. "And notice that your back is to him. I deliberately took this seat to make sure of that, on the off chance I'm wrong."

Joe nodded.

"Know your craft," Savelev said, "but don't take anything for granted."

"Well if it's okay to talk, we better get started."

"Right. You and Poppy found something. But neither of you are on assignment."

"It happened by accident."

"Tell me."

"Poppy met a former White House staffer at one of her parties that I think has something we can use, the goods on the entire administration and the president in particular."

"You've seen it?"

"He told us about it."

"Okay."

"And if the Duchess—"

Savelev held up a hand as his cell phone rang. He answered and issued instructions and hung up and smiled at Joe.

"They're waiting in the alley," the Russian said. "Come on. Let's see how sharp our friend is."

They left their unfinished coffees on the table and went out into the warm afternoon.

New York, New York. The city so nice they named it twice. Dane had visited only once before, several years ago, and the city hadn't changed much. It was still full of too many people in too small a space, but maybe that appealed to some, especially the population that thought the city was the best city on earth.

He sat in the coffee shop watching Savelev and the younger man and read almost every article in the front section of the newspaper, with only an occasional glance at the pair. He sipped hot green tea and did not blot out the noises around him. The bad music over the speakers. The jumble of customer voices. The commotion behind the counter. There was something American about the whole experience, and it was one he did not find a facsimile of anywhere else in the world.

Except for the chairs. The hard-wooden chairs always made his rear end sore, and every coffee shop in the world had the same chairs. Like they all bought from the same place.

Dane kept reading. He glanced at two photographs of current US President Peter Cross and noted that he had put on a few pounds since the last time he'd seen him. But he still looked sharp. Opponents continued to criticize him over policy decisions, specifically America's continuing conflict in the Middle East. A related article highlighted his connection with Baden-Solitron, which had only a few months earlier won a huge government contract to rebuild the portions of the Middle East where US forces played. An editorial thought the connection was too close, that the president was granting favors to a friend. The connection

should be investigated by Congress, the writer said, imply-
ing that Peter Cross was less than trustworthy. Dane only
shook his head. Cross would always help a friend. He had
helped Dane in many ways, many years ago. He would
never do anything illegal.

The writer also did not like Cross's ties with the Central
Intelligence Agency, where he'd been Director of Central
Intelligence for a number of years. It was an old gripe, but
the other side never let it go.

He cast another glance at Savelev and his younger
companion.

Savelev was dressed for casual business in light-colored
clothes and dark shoes, his hair a typical close-cropped
military cut. The younger man looked like a Wall Streeter
with too much money, an obvious Saville Row suit fit to
his trim body, but there were no muscles under the fabric.
A Rolex Sea Dweller was on the younger man's left wrist.
They stood and went out. Dane waited thirty seconds,
about as long as it took to close the paper and roll it into a
tube and followed. He carried no firearm and had a feeling
about Savelev's phone call. Even a makeshift weapon was
better than no weapon at all, so he tucked the newspaper
under his left arm.

He'd been following them for most of the morning,
not bothering with any of the typical shadowing tactics
meant to conceal. He wanted to get caught. That was the
whole point. But throughout the morning, Savelev and his
apprentice appeared not to notice him. Until, that is, they
entered the coffee shop.

The two men continued talking, Savelev using his hands
a lot. Was he Russian or Italian? What was it with people
using their hands to talk with? How hard was it to keep
the damn things still? Foolish question. The movement of

hands when talking served a unique purpose. It kept some people from going insane.

Savelev made what looked like a hand signal as they passed the mouth of an alley. Dane stepped closer to the curb, using a chatting couple for cover, and walked by the alley. The two men who emerged made the mistake of looking right at him. Amateurs. They fell in step behind him. They were young like Savelev's companion but dressed for the street.

Dane moved to the middle of the sidewalk and clutched the newspaper a little tighter.

At the next alley, he turned and sprinted a short distance to a dumpster, stood behind it, and listened to the hurried footsteps of the pair coming after him. He emerged from cover, and the two men stopped short. Steve Dane grinned. He said:

"Class is in session."

One of them dug under his coat. Dane whipped the newspaper up and back down, delivering a stinging double blow to Number One's face. As the wannabe gunfighter recoiled back, Dane swung a backspin kick into Number Two's midsection. Two flew back into the wall, dropped. Dane closed in on One, who had his gun out, and smacked his wrist with the paper, then punched him in the jaw. As One fell, the gun clattered to the pavement and Dane kicked it under the dumpster.

Number One was out cold, Number Two was groaning. Dane knelt beside Number Two and removed a pistol and tossed it. He checked the man's pockets and found a cell phone, which he slipped into his own pocket.

"Wow," said a new arrival.

Dane looked behind him and saw a homeless man rising from a shelter further down the alley. "Better than TV!"

"Glad you liked it."

"They got any money?"

Dane stood. "Go ahead and look. Be done when they wake up."

The bum laughed and shuffled toward Dane. "Nuts. I can take 'em."

Dane waved and left the alley. So far so good. The phone was a real coup. He had a surefire way of contacting Savelev now.

Chapter Thirty-Seven

Dane found a bus stop and sat on the side of the metal bench that did not have bird crap on it, and scrolled through the names on the cell and clicked on Savelev's number.

The Russian answered. His accent wasn't thick. "Success?"

"Sorry. Your people need to learn that carrying a gun doesn't mean they're invincible."

A moment of silence, then Dane heard a car horn and a man yelling something in the background. "I will keep that top of mind. Who are you?"

"Never mind. I have something you want. Something your boss wants."

"Which is?"

"An M5205."

"Nobody has one of those."

"Check your sources for a hijacking. The army is keeping it quiet."

"Whoever you are—"

"You check and call me at this number."

Dane turned off the phone. He called McConn on his

own phone. Todd had been trailing Dane but would not have hung around waiting to see if Dane needed backup. He knew as well as Dane that the two goons weren't serious trouble and had kept trailing the Russian.

McConn said, "They're still walking."

"Did they spot you?"

"Nope."

"I don't think Nina's old boss is very sharp. He's working with a bunch of nobodies."

"I saw the thugs in the alley, yeah."

"I guess we'll see just how dumb he is soon enough."

Alek Savelev paced the thick carpet in the den of his top-level apartment in the East 40s. He didn't wear shoes. The soft carpet felt good on the bottoms of his feet, a major contrast after walking on the sidewalk most of the morning.

He had a large place. Aside from the den, there was a spacious kitchen and living room, and a patio on the roof that offered an exclusive view of New York City that only he and his guests ever saw.

He said into the telephone, "I've confirmed with three sources that an M5205 was stolen, Angelica. No doubt."

"What do they say happened?" said the woman on the other end of the line. The Duchess.

"There were two trucks carrying about a dozen weapons total. They were delivering to the Special Warfare Center at Fort Bragg. Halfway there an armed group blocked the road, shot out the tires of each truck and took a crate containing one of the weapons."

"Any of the drivers shot?"

"No."

"And this guy just happened to find you?"

"It won't hurt to have a conversation. But with the

trouble we've had—"

"I know."

Savelev stopped pacing and looked out the window. A group of pigeons lined the edge of the roof. They were always there. He could shoo them away, but they always returned.

He said nothing more. Nobody disturbed the Duchess when she was thinking.

"Make the call," she said.

"Okay."

"And Alek? If your protégés are truly going to be useful, they will have to do better."

The cell phone rang. It wasn't a normal ring, but an obvious pop tune Dane did not recognize. The caller ID said ALEK, so Dane said, "Here we go," and as Nina and McConn scooted closer he answered.

"Yes?"

"When can we talk?" Savelev said.

"We leave tonight, so it has to be now."

"We?"

"I'm not alone."

"Be at my place in one hour." Savelev rattled off the address. Dane hung up.

Dane and Nina left the hotel in a cab, with McConn following behind in a second cab, and they pulled up in front of Savelev's brownstone right on time. McConn's cab dropped him off half a block away, and he found an alley from which to watch.

The young buck Dane had seen at the coffee shop greeted him and Nina at the door. He introduced himself as Joe Bradley. Dane decided he could only have been WASP-ier if his last name had been Smith or Jones. He wore the same suit, but the cuffs on his sleeves were rolled back. The Rolex gleamed.

He led them through the tiled hallway without a pat-down, giving Dane's briefcase only a cursory glance.

Joe stopped at the open double doors of a den. Alek Savelev rose from behind his desk. "Thank you, Joe," he said, and froze when he saw Nina.

"Nina?"

"Hello, Alek."

"It's been, my goodness, it's been ages."

"Only a few years, really."

"Feels like longer. Are you with him?"

"I'm the brains of the outfit."

Dane laughed.

Savelev smiled. "You always were." He crossed the room to them and hugged Nina, but her return embrace held no enthusiasm. To Dane he said, "My apologies for earlier."

"Forget it. It hurt them more than me."

"I didn't get your name."

"Dane. Steve Dane."

"Let's have a drink before we talk business." He gestured to Dane's briefcase. "Is that the weapon?" And he laughed.

Savelev poured vodka for Nina without asking, but he did ask Dane for a request. Dane pointed at a bottle of Crown Royal and asked for a double.

Drinks in hand, they sat on a couch while Savelev occupied a seat on Dane's right. The couch and the cushions were wrapped in soft black leather. Dane let his body sink into them and crossed his legs.

Savelev said, "I'm impressed with your work."

"You mean the people I hire?" Dane said.

"Of course. Maybe you can teach my team a thing or two."

"What are you up to these days, Alek?" Nina said.

"This and that."

"Stop. You're a spymaster surrounded by young people, and Americans, no less. This can't be an official job. Are you working for yourself now?"

"Much like you, I am operating on the fringes."

"Tell me," Nina said. "I'd love to hear about it. Maybe we can help each other further."

Savelev dropped his eyes and grinned into his glass.

"He doesn't want to talk about it." Dane put his glass on the table before him, lifted the briefcase to his lap and opened the case. He handed Savelev the photos inside, the pictures taken of the M5205 being tested.

Savelev put his drink down and examined the photos. They showed only Dane holding the weapon, shooting it, and the truck on fire in the background. The pics had been snapped after the first test shot.

"This could be faked," Savelev said. He cocked an eye at Dane.

Dane shrugged. "It's up to you if we go forward."

Savelev examined the photos a second time. Dane and Nina remained quiet and uninterested.

"When can I see it?"

"It can be here in two days."

Savelev handed back the pictures. "Then in two days we will talk again."

"Come on, Alek," Nina said. "We can have a lot of fun in two days. Don't be a pimple."

Savelev laughed. "Always had a way with words. Where are you staying?"

"The Ritz," she said.

"Of course, where else?" To Dane, "She drove accounting nuts. Never could stay in a normal place. It had to be top of the heap."

Dane smiled. "That's why I have to steal so much."

"There's a lot to steal in New York," Savelev said, "but sometimes the best way to steal is to let people, I don't know, give things to you."

"Let me see if I can figure this out," Nina said. "You've got a bunch of young bucks working with you…"

Savelev didn't bat an eye.

"And New York is full of diplomats…"

Savelev started to smile.

"Could what these people give you be information? You're using these kids to spy on diplomats so you can sell the information?"

"Not just diplomats," Savelev said. "There are a lot of industrial secrets to trade, too."

"They collect it and bring it to you, and you determine the value."

Savelev stood up. "Want a refill?" Nina handed him her glass. While his back was to them, Nina winked at Dane.

Savelev brought back Nina's drink and returned to his seat. "Actually, I don't have much time," he said. "I have to meet one of my people tonight. Why don't you two come along? Dinner's on me. Or, my boss, really. But she won't mind."

"There was a time you didn't want women anywhere in the field. You told me you'd make an exception. Now you're working for one?"

"I've matured," Savelev said. He smiled.

"Or she pays you enough not to care."

Dane said, "Finish your drink, dear." To Savelev, "We'd be delighted to join you. Thank you for the offer."

"I only do business with friends," the Russian said. "A toast to friendship?"

They clinked glasses.

Chapter Thirty-Eight

Poppy August painted her lips red to match her hair and flashed a white smile at the image in the glass. Her curled hair already looked great. Its color, length and sheen never failed to attract the male attention she wanted, though it also brought plenty of attention she didn't want from guys she'd never in a million years consider.

She had dressed to kill tonight. Black boots, black stockings, a tight strapless cocktail dress that showed off her carefully maintained curves. The dress was cut low enough to be tantalizing but not so low as to reveal any major image of the twins. She wasn't a tart, after all. Con artist, thief, yes, but never a whore, despite the premium she could have charged. Why did men go so bonkers over redheads, anyway?

She'd been working for Savelev for the past year after spending more years than she cared to remember working on her own. Meeting him had been a lucky break. Fate smiling at her and all that. She'd hit a dry spell as far as cons went, and a partner she'd made some good money with had checked into the nuthouse. While waiting for a new thing to turn up, she'd taken to picking pockets in Times Square. One night she picked Savelev's pocket, only he caught her, using such a powerful vice grip on her wrist that she actually cried out. But instead of calling the cops, he'd bought her coffee and interviewed her. She told him a little about her life. He had charm and displayed the signs of a kindred spirit. It took a con artist to know a con artist. At the end of their chat, Savelev said: "Join me and you can do more than make money. You can change the course of the world."

Well, there was no way to refuse a line like that!

She grabbed her coat and purse, locked the apartment and walked down the hall.

A stop-and-go cab ride took her to The Tipsy Cow, a popular new nightspot. She paid the fare, tipping with only a smile, and swished inside like she owned the place. A wall of music and noise and stuffy air struck her like a fierce wind. She powered through. Blasting past the greeter with another smile, Poppy paused when she saw Savelev at a corner table with a man and a woman she did not recognize. Savelev stood, waved her over. She took the chair Savelev offered.

"Hi," she said to the new pair. No smile this time.

Savelev said, "This is a great opportunity for you, my dear. May I present Mr. Steve Dane and Miss Nina Talikova."

Poppy finally smiled at Dane and he held her eyes, but her smile faded fast. He did not react to her. No flush up his neck or any indication that she had any effect on him. The other woman, maybe ten years older than her and with the soft lines to prove it, wore a disapproving look. The kind Mother always had even though she hadn't seen the witch since she was fifteen.

Savelev said, "Nina and I worked together in Moscow. She is what you can be."

Old and useless? "Oh," Poppy said.

The other woman winked. Poppy dropped her eyes to the table.

"When does your connection show up?" Savelev said.

Poppy turned her attention to her mentor's approving eyes. "Any minute," she said. "Gotta run," and she scooted from the table and relocated to the bar, where she ordered an Appletini, found an empty stool, and waited for her contact.

Nina leaned across the table to Savelev. "That girl is reckless."

"Why do you say that?"

"She has that look in her eyes, Alek. She's not in this for you or your money. She likes the kicks."

"If Poppy getting kicks helps me and my employer, that is not a bad thing."

"She'll get somebody killed before this is over," Nina said. "Or get killed herself."

"Steve? Your thoughts?"

Dane chewed some ice, swallowed. "I could use another drink," he said. What he didn't say was that he wanted to see what Poppy's contact was peddling, and fast. This was the first hint that the Duchess had more in mind than selling weapons. Their waitress returned, and Dane bought the next round; his eyes were never far from Poppy August.

Poppy drank some of her Appletini, scanning the crowd, blowing off two Wall Streeters who hit on her. When she saw her contact, Luke, cut through the crowd, she waved at him, bracelets tinkling like wind chimes, not that anybody could hear them over the crowd noise. He wasn't in a suit like the first time they'd met; he wore a blue button-down shirt and black slacks and leather shoes this time. The combo combined with his surfer haircut made him adorable. He hadn't worn his hair that way the first time they met, either.

She smiled at him, said, "Hey, cutie," and kissed his cheek. His body stiffened, and she frowned.

"What the hell, baby?"

He grabbed her wrists, but there was no warmth in his hands. "We gotta get out of here. I'm being followed."

"You are?"

"Come on, let's go."

"Luke, relax, I got people all over. You think I'm doing this by myself? Come and dance first." She pulled him toward the floor.

"Poppy."

She laughed. "We'll be fine!"

Another hand grabbed her arm. Hard.

Chapter Thirty-Nine

Dane said, "Those Wall Street boys are watching her."

"Could be nothing," Nina said.

"She knows they are there," Savelev said.

"Is that the contact?" Dane said.

"That's not a Republican haircut," Nina said.

"And now she's so busy trying to get him to dance, she doesn't see one of the Wall Street boys making a phone call."

"I'll start the car," Nina said. "Let's go, Alek."

The three slid out of the booth but Dane broke off, weaved through the crowd toward the bar. Poppy was pulling on her contact's arm; Dane grabbed her arm, squeezing, and she swung fiery eyes his way.

"You—"

Dane yanked her closer. The contact stared, wide-eyed.

"You're being watched," Dane said, his own eyes on the Wall Streeters. They started to rise from their table, and one reached under his coat. "Follow Savelev out the back," he said, and gave her and the contact a shove toward their former table.

The Wall Streeters closed in. One held a pistol beside his leg. Dane moved forward to intercept. He grabbed the armed man's wrist, twisting the arm behind his back, using his left hand to shove the man's head into the round edge of the bar. He pivoted with his left elbow cocked and nailed the second Wall Streeter in the jaw. Both crumpled in a heap. Witnesses gasped and pointed, but the crowd and noise covered Dane as he slipped away and out the front door.

He crossed the street to where Nina had parked at a fire hydrant, and squeezed into the back, crushing Poppy against her contact and the contact against the door.

Another dumb mistake, Dane thought. The contact should have been in the middle.

Nina drove off.

Poppy shoved back against Dane. "What the hell?"

"You almost blew it back there, party girl."

The contact said, "I tried to tell her—"

"Stow it. Do you have the goods or not?"

"Here," the contact said, and dug into his shirt pocket. He handed Dane a flash drive.

"And what do I do with this piece of plastic?" Dane said.

"Now's who's stupid?" Poppy said. She reached up her skirt, yanked an iPhone from her garter clip, took the flash drive and plugged it into the phone's side port. Turning up the volume, she played the single audio file stored on the drive. They listened to every word. They listened to the voices of President Peter Cross and another man.

"One of those guys is the President," Nina said, "but who's the other man?"

"Lee Hosler," Dane said.

"Who?"

"Wait."

It was a dull conversation to start. Dane didn't see the

value in it at all. Until—

"The company is in a real bind, Pete. I need help to keep the doors open."

"What were you thinking?"

"We could really use some new government contracts. Something long-term with cash flow, you know."

"Well maybe you've been watching the news. Things aren't going well with—well, that country that has the nukes, you know what I mean—and we're probably going to invade next week. Your company would be perfect to lead whatever rebuilding effort we put in after the fighting is done."

"Okay."

"It'll take some time, but I'll make it happen. And maybe we can wreck a few extra buildings for you too."

The chat continued for a few extra moments, and then the audio clip ended.

"Tell me," Nina said.

"Lee Hosler," Dane said. "Owner of Baden-Solitron. He's in the papers a lot. It's a construction firm that's been involved in a lot of high-profile projects. He and the President went to school together, and Hosler is a reliable source of campaign cash. There's been a lot of criticism in the press that Baden-Solitron recently got big favors from the government to rebuild the Middle East, and I guess this is how it happened. This isn't cocktail party gossip. That's why those goons were back there. Give me the earphones for this."

Poppy dug through her purse and handed Dane the small earbuds, which he plugged into the iPhone. He listened to the recording several more times. Something wasn't right, and not only the fact that Cross would never make the kind of deal the recording said he did. Yes, he would always help a friend. Trying to help Hosler get some business was right up his alley, and there was nothing illegal there. But causing more damage in the name of profit? Not Peter Cross.

He played the recording again.

The last two sentences…

"It'll take some time but"—background noise—"I'll make it happen"—more background noise, a door closing and a third voice cut off—"and maybe we can wreck a few extra buildings for you too."

The iPhone's speakers were too small to define the noise, and the average person would probably miss it, but not Dane. He'd edited enough recordings in his career to know a professional's touch when he heard it.

"It'll take some time but I'll make it happen. And maybe we can wreck a few extra buildings for you too."

No doubt it was Cross saying the words, but he hadn't said them in that order. The third person's voice really gave it away. The voice was chopped off mid-sentence, the words unintelligible, but wholly out of place in the quiet background of the rest of the chat. The recording had been digitally spliced. Cross's remarks about blowing up extra buildings might have been an opening joke; it was just like him to do that. And a political enemy with an axe to grind would know just what to do with such a line.

But he couldn't share any of this.

He pulled out the earbuds. "How did you get this?"

"Off the hard drive all of Cross's recordings are saved on," he said. "I copied it off the disk. That's the only one I have."

"You're a marked man, kid. Any idea who you're dealing with? To keep something this hot under wraps, they'll hire real muscle, and you'll never tie it back to the President."

Poppy said to the contact, "What about the rest of it?"

Dane said, "The rest of what?"

"Papers formalizing the deal," the contact said. "In a safe at Hosler's place. Signed papers proving the whole thing."

"He'll destroy any documents he has now that the audio is out," Dane said.

"Not my problem. Where's my money?"

Savelev passed back a thick envelope. Poppy took it and handed it to the contact. He ruffled through the bills inside.

Dane said, "I hear Acapulco is nice this time of year."

"I got plans. Let me off here."

Nina found a place to pull over, and the contact jumped out. No good-bye. Poppy watched him go. Her eyes looked sad, like a puppy being left behind by its owner at a kennel.

"You'll find another," Dane said.

"I hate you," she said.

Dane took a deep breath as Nina drove on. Nobody talked for the remainder of the drive. Nina parked in front of Savelev's brownstone, and they followed the Russian into the house.

Chapter Forty

Dane brought Nina a drink and joined her on the couch. Savelev
paced the floor, holding his glass, and the ice cubes in the
drink clinked together as he moved.

"Sit down, Alek," she said.

Savelev stopped and glared at her.

"Sit down," Dane told him. "Come on, relax."

Savelev sat across from them.

"I think I'll need to bring in somebody else for the rest
of this," Savelev said. "We need to break into that safe and
at least see if those papers are there."

Dane said, "Make me a deal on the M5205 and I'll bust
that safe for an extra twenty grand. You won't get a deal
like that anywhere else."

"You'd do it alone?"

"No. Nina comes with me. But you'd be a fool to
turn this down."

Savelev started to say something, paused, shook his head.

"I have the recording," he said. "I don't need what's in
the safe. Nothing is more damaging than the President's
own voice."

"There are too many ways to spin that," Dane said. "They can create doubt about the validity of a recording. The administration's opponents want all the ammo they can get to keep him from a second term, and this is exactly what they need, a president who took the country to war to line the pockets of a pal. And if those papers have signatures on them, it's all gravy."

Savelev held up a hand, and Dane stopped. The Russian spymaster downed his drink. "Finish up," he said. "I'm very tired. We'll talk again tomorrow."

Dane said nothing more, and Nina followed his lead. They finished their drinks, and Savelev showed them out. They walked two blocks before hailing a cab.

"How do you think it went?" Dane said. Nina sat beside him. Street-lights flashed on her face as the taxi powered along the road.

"Savelev will bite," she said. "But he needs to sleep on it. Why did you listen to that so many times?"

"Because that conversation was constructed."

"What do you mean?"

Dane's phone vibrated in his pocket. He answered. It was McConn. He was already back at the hotel, waiting. Dane told him they'd be there shortly.

The three met on the hotel's ninth floor observation deck. "No Smoking" signs were posted everywhere. The deck covered the length of one side of the building. Tables and chairs were spread about, with tall lamps providing illumination. The winking lights of the city sprawled before them.

Dane lit a cigar. He couldn't read.

"Did those goons have company?" he asked McConn.

"Not that I saw."

"Enough," Nina said. "Tell me why you think that recording is fake."

"Fake?" McConn said.

"There's a background noise in the end that sounds like a door closing and the words of somebody else being cut off mid-sentence. My bet is that whoever the person in the background is showed Hosler into the Oval Office and said something as he left and shut the door. Cross likes to make jokes. That line about blowing up buildings must have been his opening line. The rest of the recording is quiet up until that point, which means it took place before."

"Are you sure?" McConn said.

"I've doctored recordings to make people look bad, and I also know Peter Cross," Dane said. "I wouldn't stick my neck out for him if I thought he was dirty."

"How do you think it was doctored?" McConn said.

Dane explained: "In the old days we had to splice actual tape together, remember? Now when you load a sound file into a computer, you can edit the MP3 or whatever the format is with a sound-editing program. Some PCs come with them installed in movie-making applications. Most you have to buy or find a free one to download. When you have the file open on the screen, you can cut and paste pieces of the file the same way you'd copy and paste a text document. That's how they did the Cross recording, rearranging the elements of the conversation, but it's not perfect. You can't erase the background noise on the cheap sound file programs."

"You realize this has become more than just trying to sell the Duchess a classified military weapon?" McConn said.

"Way more than that," Dane said. "Poppy's contact pulled a really nice scam. He knows the recording is fake, and because deep down he knows the President probably still has the original, it's absolutely useless for blackmail. Those are the facts as I see them. He convinced Poppy, who convinced Savelev, that he had the genuine article. This was a scam from start to finish, and Savelev and his crew don't realize they've been taken."

"Poppy's an idiot," Nina said.

"And that contact took them for a pile of money," McConn said.

"Yup. For all we know, those goons at the bar were pals of his and in on the whole thing. The contact approached Poppy at one of her parties, remember? It may not be a secret what she's doing, with all her flash and dash. They saw an opportunity and took it."

"Is this the part where we laugh?" McConn said. "I mean, seriously—"

"This is the part where we keep playing along," Dane said, "and we keep the scam going by making them believe the Secret Service is actively looking for the recording and the people who stole it. We keep up the pressure so Savelev has no choice but to flee the country and take us straight to the Duchess."

Dane and Nina slept well into the afternoon the next day, rising after noon, and while Dane showered, Nina looked out the window of the hotel room. She didn't comprehend anything before her. Her mind was on the past, and she was glad to finally have some time to herself so she could sort through the emotions running through her. Seeing Savelev again had unleashed memories she wanted to forget very much.

Alec Savelev had thought he was helping her avenge the man she loved all those years ago when he gave her the names of three men that she could kill if she so desired.

Killing those who murdered her boyfriend had helped with the pain, at first, until she saw the consequences of shooting the trio. She never told Savelev what happened after. She didn't want him to carry the burden she felt.

He'd meant well then. He was still the same man, trying to do his best, but now for a client instead of the Motherland.

She hoped his association with The Duchess didn't lead to his death, but she also knew there might not be any choice in the matter. If it came down to him or her, or him and Dane with her in the middle, she knew where she'd send a bullet.

She turned as Dane stepped out of the shower and used one of the thin hotel towels to dry off in front of her. He didn't mind being naked in front of her. He didn't mind that she saw his burn scars from top to bottom. He hid from others, but not from her. Only with her could he be fully transparent.

And yet she kept secrets from him. Not because she didn't want him to know, but because she was trying to protect herself.

As he tied on a blue robe, she said, "Alek called."

"Did you talk to him?"

"Let it go to voicemail."

"Okay." Dane brushed by her and she went into the bathroom.

"I hope you didn't use all the hot water," she said.

"This isn't Siberia, baby."

"Keep up comments like that and I'll cut you off again."

"And your resolve will quickly weaken," he said, "because you can't say no to an amazing specimen like me."

"I've managed once already!" She slammed the door.

Dane laughed and shook his head. Sometimes she bested him in the banter no matter how hard he tried. He ordered lunch from room service, pulled on his clothes and sat out on the deck with the patio door cracked. He stood at the rail and listened to the city. The heartbeats of passing cars and buses were loud even at this height.

Room service knocked and Dane answered. A blonde-haired kid wheeled in a cart loaded with covered silver trays. Dane sent him away with a nice tip. He set the plates on the table. Kobe beef hamburgers on French rolls, even though one could not get "real" Kobe beef in the States. Only Japan had the real deal, but US beef manufacturers did their best to imitate it and priced it accordingly. It wasn't as good as the real thing, but it was good. Dane had requested that none of the usual "fixin's" be added. One aspect of the meat was that it had enough flavor to not require any kind of modification.

Nina exited the bathroom, tossed her PJs on the bed and, still dripping a little, grabbed an outfit and returned to the bathroom to dress. By the time she joined Dane at the table, he was three bites ahead.

"Your phone rang again," he said.

"Alek?"

"I didn't bother to look."

"He's taking the bait."

"Probably. He can wait until we finish."

Chapter Forty-One

"I want Poppy to go with you."

"No way."

They sat at a table on the upper patio of Savelev's place. He'd hosed off the concrete prior to their arrival; the air smelled wet. The ever-present pigeons had been on the roof's edge when they took their seats, but quickly flew to the top edge of the neighboring building—waiting to see what scraps of food the larger creatures left behind.

"I want her at a professional level. She's the best of the pack. You're the only one who can train her properly."

"Because I'm a woman?"

"Once she sees what you're capable of, she won't be able to get enough. Show her everything you know. Like I showed you."

"If she's the best you have," Nina said, "it's nothing to brag about. The answer is still no."

"You want to see the Duchess," Savelev said. "You cannot get to her without my help."

"And you want us to rob a safe," Nina said. "We don't have to do that. Don't forget that we can sell the weapon elsewhere."

Savelev and Nina locked eyes. Dane looked from one to the other, noting the sharp set to their jaws and un-blinking eyes. This kind of argument was nothing new to them. He didn't want Poppy tagging along either, but this was the best lead they had to the Duchess, and they couldn't risk wrecking it.

It helped that Nina said no. If they went along too willingly, Savelev would sense a fast one.

The Russian said to Dane, "What do you think?"

"Yes, honey, what do you think?"

Dane couldn't fight the grin that spread across his face. "She can join us."

Nina shook her head.

Savelev clapped his hands and let a laugh. "Good! Now let's look at some pictures of Hosler's house." He left the table and went inside.

Nina leaned close. "I was serious."

"I know. That's why he believed you."

"She's nothing but trouble and you know it."

"And we've fallen pretty far if we can't handle her."

"We'll be armed. She'll have a gun. How do you propose to handle that?"

"I have a plan."

"Do you?"

Savelev returned and Nina sat up. She did not look directly at him as he rejoined the table and handed Dane some pictures.

The pictures showed Hosler's mansion, placed in the center of an open field. Security men, some with dogs, dotted the property.

"This is it?" Dane said. "No pictures of the safe? How do I know what I'm breaking into?"

"We couldn't get that close," Savelev said. "The safe is in Hosler's study, and his study is on the ground floor. See there?" He pointed at one picture that showed a sliding glass door off a small patio. "The safe is there, I swear."

"This isn't as thorough as I'd like," Dane said.

"Best we could do."

Nina said, "Your people do need help. A lot of it."

Nina said, "She's going to drag us down."

They were back at the hotel.

"Poppy already knows how to handle a gun, so we don't have to show her that. But we need to make sure we check her gear. Tomorrow morning, find a gun shop that sells blanks and make sure they're loaded in Poppy's gun."

"That's rich."

"You got a better idea?"

"What about the rest?"

"Hosler has security but we can't kill anybody."

"They'll be trying to kill us."

"Exactly. So, we shoot to wound only. We'll put McConn in the trees with a rifle to provide covering fire. While the three of you keep the security force occupied, I'll slip into the house."

"Think Hosler will be there?"

"I hope he is. I'd like to have a word with him."

The night of the break-in, they left the car five miles from the estate. They were dressed head to toe in black with beanie caps and face paint to complete the commando ensemble. Dane carried a leather satchel across his chest that contained needed tools for cracking the safe, with extra room for the boodle when he found it. The gear was a ploy in case Poppy told Savelev about it. He would not touch any of those tools.

Hiking through the forest, Dane, Nina and Poppy came to a hill overlooking the property. A narrow clearing provided space for them to drop prone and begin observations. The ground was soft and cold, and the chill bit through their clothes. They'd warm up again once the action started.

Something scurried up a nearby tree trunk, across the upper branches, shaking the leaves. Steve Dane paid no attention. He knew a squirrel when he heard one. But Poppy August was not so accustomed, and she tried to follow the sound with her eyes.

Hosler's property contained a small stable of horses, a pool, and a garden. As estates went, it was pretty modest, and trees and shrubbery, especially near the house, provided ample cover and concealment. Dane scanned the property with night-vision binoculars. Patrolmen crisscrossed the field in fifteen-minute intervals. It did not appear that there were many of them, but more could have been hanging out inside.

He lowered the binoculars and let out a breath.

"What's wrong?" Nina said.

"Alek's recon photos showed more men."

"Is he gone? That might help us."

"Assuming he hasn't taken the file with him."

"Why would he go on the road and risk losing the file in transit? A portable safe isn't a safe at all."

"And if he's gone and left a large force behind, we're walking into a mess."

Poppy said, "We're still going, right?"

Dane said yes. They didn't have another option, but his gut told him to tread carefully. He checked his watch. In seven minutes McConn would start his part of the plan. Dane had no way of contacting his friend, but they'd agreed on a time to begin the proceedings. At the appointed time, if guards were out, McConn would, from his hiding spot and with a scoped rifle, shoot however many he could.

"Move out," Dane said.

He broke off alone, following the slope to the fence, then running along the fence to the opposite side of the house where they knew Hosler's study to be.

Nina rose and headed straight for the fence, placing her steps without haste, making no sound. Poppy snapped twigs and rustled branches. The fence was made of wood, with horizontal boards stacked three high and separated by gaps; Nina pulled the HK close to her body and rolled under the fence. Poppy tried to duplicate the move but got stuck when the barrel of her HK bumped the bottom plank of the fence. She adjusted and rolled up beside Nina.

"Takes practice," Nina said, and moved ahead in a quick trot. But then her foot struck something hard and she dropped face first into the grass.

Floodlights blazed to life but no alarms sounded.

"What's this?"

Nina pushed up, looked back. Poppy pointed at a circular metal object partially sticking out of the ground. Black plastic strips began at the top of the object and then went beneath the grass. Not a land mine.

Armed security men raced toward them.

"A motion sensor," she said. "Lock and load, honey, here they come."

Chapter Forty-Two

Todd McConn watched the property from his own night-vision scope mounted atop his semi-auto Springfield M1A. He watched Steve Dane hustle across the field, keeping to the shadows. When floodlights lit the opposite side, he didn't hesitate. He bolted from his perch, sprinting along the circular route plotted earlier that allowed a near 360-degree view of the estate. When he reached the next perch, he dropped prone, resting the rifle on a log, and switched off the night scope for a normal view. He lined up on Nina and the other woman as they readied their weapons; scanning further along, he counted three gunmen running their way. Aiming ahead of the lead gunner, he fired one shot. Nina would know the source and get out of the line of fire. The round connected, and the lead man pitched forward and landed in the grass. McConn watched him roll over and saw the leg wound. A clean hit. *Sorry, pal, just business.* Nina and Poppy fired on the other two, the muzzles of the HKs flashing in McConn's eyepiece. The shooters dropped and rolled. McConn selected the right-hand target and fired. The shot pinned the gunman to the ground. A shoulder wound this time.

A cloud of smoke drifted across the field. Nina, letting off one of her smoke grenades. He nailed the third gunman in the left arm, and a follow-up scan to the immediate left revealed more gunners racing to the scene. As Nina and Poppy ran for better cover, McConn zeroed in on the new targets and squeezed the trigger. He couldn't hit them all, but he could keep them pinned down and away from the women.

He hoped Dane was having better luck.

Poppy heard each of her heartbeats as the three gunmen closed in.

"Lock and load, honey…"

It was a line from a movie, she thought, flicking off the HK's safety like she'd been taught. Her vision clouded; sound faded. What she heard had a faint echo to it.

She lined up her sights. Or tried to. With her impaired vision, the sight picture looked nothing like it did at the range. Her pulse quickened and her breath came in short, sharp gasps. She jerked back the trigger. The HK bucked against her shoulder. Somehow the recoil didn't feel right. It was too light. She fired again. The approaching gunmen kept coming. This was a nightmare. Her bullets did nothing. The monsters kept coming. A scream caught in her throat and then—

The gunman in front seemed to—trip? She watched him fall forward and hit the ground, but also saw that one of his legs was covered in blood. Who had fired?

She glanced at Nina, who fired another burst, steady, no panic, like she was swatting a fly. Poppy jerked her head back, sighted, and fired. The muzzle flash made her wince. Still none of the gunmen dropped. She aimed for another only to see a bullet hit from another direction, ripping into the man's arm.

"Come on!" Nina shouted. It sounded like she had screamed in Poppy's ear. Poppy watched Nina pull the pin from a smoke grenade and roll it across the grass. As the thick white cloud spread, Nina ran toward the house. Poppy followed. She did not get shot in the back.

Dane heard the sharp cracks of gunfire but did not stop. His people knew what to do. He rounded a corner and stepped onto a covered patio. Through the sliding doors he spotted Hosler at his desk talking furiously on the phone. Dane advanced and smashed through the glass with the stock of the HK. Hosler dropped the phone and lunged for an open drawer. Dane blasted the phone with a single burst. The pieces landed on the carpet. Dane closed in, bits of glass that stuck to his clothes dropping off as he moved. As Hosler turned around with the gun he'd taken from the drawer, Dane stopped with the smoking muzzle of the HK mere inches from the other man's face.

"Toss it," Dane said.

"That sounds like a good idea," Hosler said. He flung the semi-automatic over the desk. It clunked on the floor.

Hosler filled his lungs with air, exhaled. He had no hair and a jowly face, but his roly-poly frame had some muscle under it. He scanned Dane's face. Recognition filled his eyes.

"Dane!" he said. "Are you behind—"

"Give me some credit."

"But—"

"I'm working with the responsible party, yes. You're lucky I convinced them to let me loot your safe."

"But the shooting—"

"You hired professionals. My people are the ones taking the risk."

"I don't understand what's going on! What do your people think they have? Pete and I didn't—"

"They have a doctored recording that makes it sound like you and Peter have conspired to profit from the war. Did he keep the original?"

"You'd have to ask him. I know he doesn't keep the recordings very long. He was stunned when he learned of the theft. There's nothing compromising on any—"

"Tell him to keep the original. If I fail, it's the only thing that will save his neck. The opposition will try and blackmail him with it, trust me."

"But why are you here now?"

"They think you have papers in your safe backing up the deal you made with Peter. I volunteered to come here and steal it."

"But Dane there's *nothing*—"

"I need to bring *something* back."

"A stack of papers, maybe? Miscellaneous items? Like you didn't have time to sort? It won't be your fault there's nothing valuable in it."

"Perfect."

It took less than two minutes to gather miscellaneous documents and a bound ledger—"Last year's take," Hosler said—and Dane stuffed it all into the leather satchel over his chest. "I don't need any of it back."

Dane went to the window. "Give the President my regards. I'll contact you somehow if I lose control of this."

"Good luck."

Dane slipped out.

Chapter Forty-Three

"Ohmygodohmygod what a rush! How did I do? Come on, be honest!" Poppy could not stay in her seat, jumpy and jittery and loud too.

"You'll get better," Nina said.

"Is it always like that? I mean I couldn't breathe or see too good, and everything had a weird echo and my gun didn't feel right—"

"Poppy. Stop. Now."

Poppy blinked at Dane and sat back. But the smile did not leave her face. "That was better than sex!"

Dane dropped Poppy off at her building. The HKs and other gear remained in the trunk; Poppy didn't ask for it. She would never see the unused blanks still in her gun.

Dane drove off and savored the silence.

Back at the hotel, Nina went to bed while Dane smoked a cigar on the deck and reviewed the night. How best to keep the pressure on Savelev? Another grin pulled at the corners of his mouth as the solution came to mind. He made a brief phone call to his CIA pal Len Lukavina. Lukavina complained about the late hour and the short notice, but after Dane explained the situation, the CIA man agreed to put a surveillance team on Savelev's place—but he also said he would have to consult higher authority. Dane had no problem with that, since Hosler would tell Cross and Cross would put the word out that Dane was to receive all the help required.

After he finished the cigar and cleaned his teeth, Dane decided that once again even a small plan beat no plan at all. And the arrangement with Lukavina would help reduce the amount of enemy personnel he had to face.

Dane crawled into bed beside a snoring Nina and quickly went to sleep.

Dane looked out the front window of Savelev's home and wondered which of the two "delivery vans" within sight was watching the place. The white vans were blank on either side. Such an obvious ruse. He wasn't in a position to complain, but one would think somebody with Lukavina's resources might do better. Maybe the second van would throw off suspicion. Crazier things had happened.

Alek Savelev sat at a table reviewing the contents of the leather satchel. He scanned each document with a growing frown. Presently he pushed the papers aside.

"That's everything?" the Russian said.

"I emptied the safe."

"It's not there. Do you think he moved the file elsewhere?"

"He would have had plenty of time."

"Unfortunate. Do you think we have what we need with just the recording? They can't spin it away, like you said?"

"They'll try. They may even succeed a little, but maybe it will inject enough poison into public opinion that the administration won't survive."

Savelev nodded. "You did well. I suppose I owe you some money."

"I didn't accomplish the mission."

"I didn't say your payment depended on getting the file. I hired you to go in and crack the safe."

Dane followed the Russian into the study, where he opened a drawer and removed a battered lock box, which he placed on the desktop and opened via a combination. Savelev raised the lid. Nestled inside with wrapped US greenbacks was the flash drive. Dane stifled a smile. Savelev truly believed he had something important. He counted out twenty one-thousand-dollar bills, severely reducing the size of the overall roll, closed the lid, put the box back in the desk.

The Russian smiled and handed the cash to Dane, who folded the bills and slipped them into his front shirt pocket. "And now the second part of our bargain."

"Indeed, my friend. I have already left a message with my employer, and she will call back before the day ends. Meanwhile I have a meeting with my team. I hope you'll excuse me."

"You don't want me and Nina here for that?"

"Not for this one."

Dane said okay. Savelev showed him out. Dane again glanced at the delivery vans. He turned right at the sidewalk and went three blocks before hailing a cab to take him back to the hotel.

Dane stood on the deck of the hotel room as the sun set. Twilight turned to evening. Nina, arms folded, leaned against the railing beside him. She said, "He's late."

Dane's cell rang. He answered and said, "Are you here? Good, come on up."

A few minutes later, Len Lukavina knocked on the door and Dane let him in. The CIA man carried a blue tote bag. They sat on the deck chairs, though Nina remained at the rail. Dane poured Crown Royal for everybody, brought Lukavina up to date.

When Dane finished, Lukavina said, "After we spoke yesterday, I got another call that about knocked me over. I've been told from the top—the tippy, tippy top, Steve—to give you everything you need."

Dane smiled. "Good old President Cross. Been watching the brownstone?"

"Of course. Saw you there. The redhead visited before you did, by the way. We've photographed three others, all male, as well."

"Round them up. Make a grab for the redhead but let her go. I need her to warn Savelev. That will clear the way for me and Nina to be their assistance in time of need."

"We can't do that," Lukavina said. "FBI will scream. There's been no time to properly investigate—"

"I don't care if you let everybody go after twenty-four hours. They're small fry. They're nothing without Savelev. We need Savelev to take us to the Duchess."

"What about McConn?"

"Keep him with you. He knows the players, so he'll come in handy."

"One condition," Lukavina said.

"Which is?"

"You wear new shoes." Lukavina set down his glass and opened the tote bag. He extracted a pair of black leather dress shoes and passed them over. Dane examined the footwear with a frown.

"Homing device in each heel," Lukavina said. "About the size of a fingernail. If I'm doing your dirty work, I want to know where you are at all times."

"Fair enough."

"Put 'em on," the CIA man said.

Dane complied and took a few steps around the deck. "Perfect fit."

"Make sure they stay on, Steve."

"Even in bed?"

"In bed, in the shower, everywhere."

Nina laughed.

Chapter Forty-Four

The next call came around nine-thirty. Nina muted the TV Dane let the phone ring two more times and then answered:

"Alek?"

"Do you have a car?" The Russian spoke fast, in a panic.

"Yeah."

"I'm with Poppy. I need you to pick us up. Don't go near the house."

"Wait, what's going on?"

"My people have been arrested. They almost got Poppy."

"Did you leave anything behind? They'll tear your place apart."

"I have everything important."

"Okay. Where are you?"

Savelev told him. Dane hung up and called Lukavina, who gave him the location of a black Chevy SUV with special CIA upgrades. A code pressed into a keypad installed on the door unlocked the vehicle. The keys were under the driver's floor mat. The supercharged motor was a plus, as was the armored glass.

With Nina in the passenger seat, Dane drove to the gas station where Savelev and Poppy were waiting, and they jumped in. Dane sped off.

Savelev, breathless, said, "Thank you."

"Anything for a pal," Dane said. "There's a motel about thirty miles up the interstate. We can go there, unless you have another idea."

"Every hideout I have is probably compromised."

Dane glanced at Poppy in the rearview. She clutched her purse to her chest and stared out the window. She shut her eyes and then opened them again. The glazed stare remained. Almost getting arrested was not, apparently, better than sex.

With evening traffic, it took over an hour to get out of the city. Dane didn't talk. He wanted Savelev and Poppy to try to relax. A tall order. But he and Nina stayed silent, and the other two watched the passing scenery. Once on the interstate, Dane opened the throttle and drove the next 30 miles at the speed limit.

Then Dane said, "How did they get onto you, Alek?"

"I don't know." The Russian spoke quietly, but the panic in his voice was gone. "We messed up somewhere. Or they grabbed Poppy's contact and he talked. It doesn't matter."

"What do your people know?" Nina said.

"Almost everything."

"Do you have any contingency plan to get out of the country?"

"Out of the *country?*" Poppy said.

"Poppy—"

"You can't be serious!"

"This is the real thing, little girl," Nina said. "Espionage will get you executed or a long prison term."

"Oh my god," Poppy said. She slumped against the

door. She let her head bump the window.

Savelev patted her leg. She inched away from him.

"I'm not worried about our exit," Savelev said. "What I am worried about is our other deal. Can you deliver the weapon like you promised?"

"All it will take is a phone call. Nina and I can get you two to the country of your choice as well."

"You know this motel you're taking us to?"

"Nope. For all I know they won't even have rooms for us. We're flipping a coin. Best we can do right now."

Savelev rubbed the right side of his face. "Okay."

Dane and Nina exchanged a glance, but neither betrayed a thought. Dane turned back to the road. As plans went, this one could not have been going better—so far. Unless Sean McFadden was with the Duchess in the dragon's lair, and then all bets were off.

They arrived at the motel and took adjoining rooms—Nina and Poppy took one, while Dane and Savelev unpacked in the other.

Savelev surveyed the room, "I guess when you're on the run, you take what you can get."

"Be grateful there isn't an accordion player nearby."

"What do you mean?"

"Forget it," Dane said.

The television was bolted to the wall; the telephone and remote control were bolted to the nightstand; the beds looked lumpy and the bedspread appeared thin. The cheesy paintings on the wall weren't worth looking at, and patches of the carpet were flat from previous foot traffic. It wasn't the Ritz. It wasn't a level or two down from the Ritz. It wasn't the bottom of the barrel, but close.

Savelev placed his bags on the bed and went into the bathroom. Dane called McConn, keeping things vague.

McConn had linked up with Lukavina and was up to speed. They talked about travel arrangements, and McConn promised that a CIA jet would be at their disposal. McConn said that the homing devices were working, and they had him pinpointed and would hang back until further notice.

The toilet flushed.

"Gotta run," Dane said. He hung up.

Savelev joined Dane at the writing table. "You didn't bring any liquor, did you?"

"Left it behind. There's a place up the road."

"I think I'll take a walk."

"Okay."

"I can trust you to watch my gear?"

"You can trust me. Not sure about Nina, though." Dane grinned.

Savelev let out weak laugh and stood up. "I shall return, my friend." He went out, pulling the door quietly shut.

Dane went outside and lit a cigar. He watched Savelev walk toward the street.

A door opened behind him. Nina stepped out.

"Where's Poppy?" Dane asked.

"In the shower. Where's Alek going?"

"For booze. He says."

"What do you mean?"

"He's testing us. Are we going to run off with his crap or not? The joke's on him."

"Uh-huh. And the bigger joke is on us if McFadden—"

"We'll find out if he'll feed us to the sharks soon enough."

"Alek won't have that recording on him. We still need to find that. Even if it's hidden somewhere, you don't want to risk anybody ever finding it, do you?"

"We'll find it."

"We may have another problem, too."

"Poppy?"

"She says if she has to run, she's going on her own."

"How big is the window in the bathroom?"

"Not big enough."

"Did you explain we won't just let her go?"

"Sure. She doesn't care."

"That's our girl," Dane said.

"I think we can use her."

Dane nodded. "If the proper moment comes, don't let it slip by."

Nina nodded and shifted her eyes from him.

"What's wrong?" he said.

"I didn't tell you the whole story between me and Alek."

"Did you two have an affair?"

"Heavens no," she said, looking back at him. "I think he wanted one, though. He helped me find some people once. You know."

"No, I don't. Hon, there's a lot you won't talk about, and I think that's why you drink so much."

"*Don't.*"

"Then tell me the story. Are you afraid we'll have to hurt Savelev?"

"Yes."

"What did he do?"

Nina shook her head and remained silent.

Dane contained his frustration. There was no sense in arguing further. When Nina decided she wasn't going to talk, she didn't say a word.

"What you're really saying is," he said, "that you'd hate to kill him."

"Yes."

"We may not have a choice, babe."

Nina let out a sigh. "I know."

Chapter Forty-Five

Savelev returned with a couple of bottles of whiskey, and the four gathered in one room to pass the hooch and take the edge off before going to bed.

Nina switched off the lamp and scooted under the covers. The bed was cold. No Steve to help warm it up. Sleeping alone wasn't fun. She rolled onto her right side.

Poppy said, "Can I tell you something?"

Nina rolled to the left but did not turn on the light. A low glow from the walkway lights outside filtered through the closed drapes. "What?"

"I can't go with you. I wasn't kidding earlier."

"You don't have a choice right now, Poppy."

"Tell me what to do. You should know all about lying low, changing your identity, all that spy stuff."

"What will you do with your new life?"

"I sure as well can't keep doing what I've been doing. All I wanted was some fun, but now look at us. Could I really be executed for this?"

"I don't make a habit of telling lies," Nina said. "Look up the Walker spy ring or Aldrich Ames. You'd probably only get life in prison, though."

"What can I do? This isn't like running a con or anything where I didn't need papers or ID cards or things like that."

"You never had the cops chasing you?"

"Nobody that I couldn't get away from using my smile. This is the friggin' government we're talking about. With heat like this, you boogey and talk later."

Nina switched on the light. The young woman, covers pulled up to her neck, made eye contact. "Stick with Steve and me. If we can't clear your name entirely, we'll get you set up somewhere. You can't do it on your own. You don't have the experience. But if you waste your new life partying—"

"No way. I'm done with that. I don't quite see myself as a working girl, but I suppose I can adapt."

"Get some rest. We'll sort it out." She turned off the light again and rolled over. She and Steve needed any ally they could get, even one like Poppy August. If they could keep her on their side, maybe dealing with the Duchess wouldn't be the death sentence she thought it was.

Dane lay in bed staring at the ceiling. The bed was actually warm despite the questionable covers. His mind raced with possible options, but no new ideas came. He had to face McFadden. He wanted the Duchess at the end of his gun. The fight had gone on long enough. He had never been a fan of just barreling into something without taking precautions, but this time it seemed like the only way.

Savelev started to snore. Dane glanced at the clock and waited another fifteen minutes and the snoring continued. He put his feet on the floor and crossed the carpet to the dresser beside the television. He rooted through a black bag but found no lock box. He did find Savelev's iPhone. Of course, he had a code Dane needed to tap in order to unlock the screen, and he was constantly surprised by how many people didn't keep their tap codes from view. Dane had watched Savelev use his code several times. He missed it on the first try, but the second unlocked the phone. Dane took it into the bathroom, where he sat on the toilet lid and scrolled through. There was no contact list or recently dialed calls. Savelev apparently dialed everything from memory and erased the record at the end of each day.

Dane flushed and left the bathroom and dropped the phone back in the bag. He added the bank address to his own phone before crawling back under the covers.

Savelev continued to snore.

The next morning, Poppy zipped her suitcase closed and was about to place it by the door when Nina stopped her.

"I want you to have this," she said, and handed the redhead a compact 9mm Glock. Her spare.

Poppy took the pistol in both hands. "You trust me?"

Heck no, Nina thought. But the little girl needed a life-line, and Nina was happy to provide it and cement Poppy's need for her and Dane.

"Don't let anybody know you have it. Even Alek."

"He was in love with you once," Poppy said. "He told me."

"I know."

"Do you think—"

"Because he brought you along, yes. The others are going to talk, but I think you know more than all of them combined. You would have been the most damaging witness. If he wasn't in love with you, he'd have left you behind."

Poppy blinked a few times. "I'm not much for relationships anyway. Guys get too clingy."

The younger woman stowed the Glock in her purse.

"Let's get breakfast," Nina said.

The four ate at a neighboring diner, and Dane outlined their travel plans. He had to laugh at how closely he was working with the Agency again. The travel plans had been made with Agency contacts and aircraft. Lukavina and McConn would be close behind every step of the way.

As she ate, Poppy kept her eyes down. She made no comment or asked any questions. Only Savelev talked at the end.

"When do we leave?"

"Anytime," Dane said. "The pilots are only waiting to hear where we're going."

"Ever been to Finland?"

"Once or twice."

"We'll land at the airport at Helsinki and then take a chopper up the gulf to where my employer is waiting. Leave the chopper arrangements to me."

"She's on one of the islands in the gulf?"

"Yes."

Dane covered his thoughts with a mouthful of corned beef hash and egg yolk. He did not like the idea of being stuck on an island but did not appear to have a choice. If that's where the Duchess was, that's where he would go.

"What kind of accommodations does your plane have? It's a long flight."

Dane grinned at Savelev. "Leather seats, satellite television, phone service and liquor for twelve."

"Who else is going?"

"Oh, just us."

Savelev laughed.

Two hours later, Dane and his companions boarded the Cessna Mustang and deposited their baggage in any available space. As everybody else sank into the plush leather swivel chairs, Dane scanned the tan carpeting with nervous eyes. The jet was part of the regular CIA fleet, but because of its side-mounted engines, an agent could not parachute out the door without getting sucked into the turbines. What CIA engineers had done to compensate was install a motorized trap door in the bottom of the planes for agents to jump from should there be a need for such activity. The plane had all the hallmarks of government inefficiency. Buying a plane with the engines under the wings would have been too damn easy. A drawback to the modification was that often there were lines cut into the carpet to cover the trap, but not this time. Lukavina and his boys had thought ahead and covered the trap with what looked like entirely new carpet. A nice touch.

Dane found a chair and strapped in. The cockpit door opened, and the copilot stepped out, and Dane did a double-take. The copilot, complete with the uniform of white shirt and black slacks of all pilots, was Todd McConn.

He grinned at Dane and spoke to everybody else. "All buckled up? We're taking off in a few minutes." The jet lurched as the pilot began to taxi. McConn grabbed the doorframe. "Damn, Harvey, let me sit down first."

"That's Captain Harvey to you," the pilot replied.

McConn shut the door.

Dane glanced over at Nina and shrugged.

Within five minutes they were in the air, and the dull throb of the quad engines filled the cabin. Dane mixed four whiskey and sodas to get everybody comfortable.

The best they could do for food was an assortment of pre-made sandwiches or frozen dinners. After a few hours Dane and Nina served up the eats. Dane refilled the glasses and proposed a toast. He said, "To a terrific escape, and our future business together." He winked at Nina.

"I can't thank you two enough," Savelev said.

"No problem," Dane said.

"We are a good team, aren't we?" the Russian said.

Dane smiled.

Part V:
Meet the Duchess

Chapter Forty-Six

They landed at Helsinki International and taxied to a private hanger. McConn opened the exit door and thanked everybody for flying with them. He even complimented Dane's shoes. Dane wanted to punch him in the nose.

Once on the ground, Savelev took over. He made a phone call as they approached the terminal, and a customs officer met the plane at the door, brought the passengers into a private room and inspected and stamped their passports. No fuss, no delay. Dane raised an eyebrow at Savelev, who only smiled.

They followed the Russian out of the terminal to another hanger, where a chopper waited. Dane said, "I've never gone through customs that fast, anywhere in the world."

"Compliments of my employer."

All four squeezed aboard the helicopter. The pilot lifted off and flew east across the length of the airport. The cut of the gulf lay in the distance.

Dane watched the sprawling city below. The only thing separating him from being a red spot on the ground was the thin metal of the chopper's body and a piece of Plexiglas.

He felt his sweat turn cold. Maybe he didn't like small aircraft, he decided. The ride wasn't bumpy, and that made the cramped conditions more bearable.

The pilot steered left and followed the waterway. They passed over boats and the small islands that dotted the gulf. The larger land mass on the opposite side was an extension of the city. The pilot flew straight ahead. Another island in the distance grew larger as they neared, and the pilot made a circle over it. The island was covered with forest but included a large multi-level mansion on top of a hill. The roof of the mansion poked through puffs of green. Behind the mansion rose another hill, the perfect rear guard for the place. The pilot circled for a landing on a helipad located on the western side. Just before touchdown, Dane spotted a jetty on the southern side lined with small boats.

This is where the final battle would take place. It had been a long road. Italy. Paris. Mexico. New York. Friends and allies sacrificed in the struggle. A lot of scars and deeper wounds. And now the prize. If they could take it. Butterflies stirred in Dane's stomach. If they could take it indeed.

The chopper descended onto the helipad. Near an arched doorway a few steps off the pad stood a man and a woman.

Nina clamped a hand on Dane's wrist and squeezed. Hard. She saw the same thing he did. The woman, they did not know. Presumably she was the Duchess. The man was Sean McFadden.

The woman was tall, hippy and busty, dark-haired, with smoldering dark eyes and a set to her jaw that left her lips a flat line. She stood with folded arms in a blue dress and black boots.

As Dane climbed out of the chopper, he saw McFadden whisper in her ear.

Dane helped Nina out of the helicopter, instinctively

bending at the waist to avoid the whipping rotors overhead despite the blades' being high enough. They hung back while Savelev hustled around the back of the chopper and, leading Poppy by the arm, approached the Duchess.

"Hello, Angelica," he said. She offered her cheek and he pecked it.

He introduced Poppy, and the Duchess nodded curtly at the redhead. He introduced Dane and Nina, and the Duchess smiled. A little.

"I have heard a lot about you," the Duchess said, making no move to shake hands. "I am Angelica Kyznetsov. You already know the other name I'm known by."

She spoke with no trace of an accent.

She said, "My number two, Sean McFadden," and gestured to him. As usual his dark hair was slicked back. He wore a gray sweater and blue jeans. "He's my all-around troubleshooter."

McFadden shook hands, and Dane caught the smirk McFadden tried to hide. Dane stepped back. The next move was Sean's.

The Duchess led them through the doorway. Inside stood a pair of guards. She asked the guards to escort the guests to their rooms.

Dane and Nina had a large bedroom with a king bed and private bathroom. Cream-colored walls, muted colors. Nothing too fancy, nothing bolted down. The window offered a partial view of Helsinki and highlighted the black waters of the gulf, which looked like a huge gap of space between danger and safety. The chopper ride had taken less than ten minutes, but Dane felt very far away.

They dropped their suitcases on the bed and immediately removed their handguns from the X-ray-proof bottoms of each case.

"How long before McFadden talks?" Nina said.

"He might be talking right now. Or he might not be."

"You still think—"

Somebody knocked on the door. Dane reached for the knob while Nina stepped to one side with her Smith & Wesson M&P Shield in hand and her finger on the trigger.

Dane opened the door. "Yes?"

One of the guards who had escorted them to the room stood in the hall.

"The Duchess wants you both," the man said, "for dinner at eight. I'll be back to get you at a quarter till."

Steve Dane stared at the man a moment. "Okay." He closed the door. He turned back to Nina. She put away her gun.

"I hope she can cook," Nina said.

"I'll settle for the food not being poisoned," Dane said.

Smoked salmon served in a cream sauce and accompanied by russet potatoes and steamed vegetables. Dane ate without hesitation. Anybody who would poison such a wonderful spread had no respect for food.

"I like simple food," the Duchess said.

Dane and Nina sat beside each other on one side of the table, and on the other sat Savelev and Poppy. At either end sat the Duchess and Sean McFadden. Light music played through hidden speakers. The dining room had light-paneled walls and carpeting. A bright chandelier, jeweled and sparkling, hung from above.

The Duchess sipped a glass of red wine, and for the first time Dane saw the bulged knuckles of her right hand.

His eyes lingered a little too long.

The Duchess set down her glass. "They're the one deformity I have, Mr. Dane. But I wasn't born with them."

"I didn't mean to stare."

"I'm not offended." She held up the hand. "This hand was slammed in a drawer by one of my early employers who did it to teach me a lesson. I'd botched a job. A simple one, they told me. Like a lot of things, it turned complicated very quickly and my employers did not understand the choices I had to make."

"Sounds familiar."

"I waited until my hand healed and then struck back. He should have expected it, but he thought I was just a silly bitch. I poisoned his coffee one morning, and he died horribly. Then I took over the organization, and that's how the Duchess was born."

"How long have you been in business? We never heard of you until recently."

Dane spoke the words carefully as he ate, marveling that she wore no glove to cover her hand. She wore the wound like a badge of honor, and the story that went with it said more about her than any dossier could ever tell.

"Two or three years," she said. "We always managed to stay under the radar until we tried selling equipment to al-Qaeda. Then somebody noticed."

"I'll say."

"I've never heard of you either, Mr. Dane."

Was that true?

"Nina and I are still under the radar."

The Duchess laughed. Savelev jumped in. "I for one am glad he and Nina turned up when they did."

"How does it feel to work with Alek again, Miss Talikova?"

"Just like the old days," Nina said.

The conversation continued but Dane tuned out. He ate

quickly, hungrier than he realized. He wiped his mouth and glanced down the table at Sean McFadden. The Irishman raised his glass Dane's way and drank down the wine.

"Mr. Dane," the Duchess said, "I suppose we should talk business. You have something I want to buy, but I don't intend to pay too much."

"Of course not."

"What is your lowest price?"

"Two million American."

"No."

"I don't intend to take a loss. It took a lot to get my hands on the M5205 and there are still people I need to pay."

"I won't give you two million."

"I can't sell it for less, and there are people who will pay much more."

"But you're here with me. You're on my property. Nobody saw you arrive. Nobody will see you leave."

"If you think that's true, you're very naive, ma'am."

Savelev dropped his fork. It clanged on his plate.

The Duchess pushed her plate aside, put her elbows on the table and rested her hand on her entwined fingers.

"How long will it take to get the item here?"

"It's already in Helsinki. I just need to make a call."

"Okay. You have a deal. Tomorrow morning. After breakfast."

Chapter Forty-Seven

Dane and Nina returned to their room, and Dane took a cigar from his travel case. As he clipped the end, somebody knocked on the door.

"Again?" he said. He lit the stogie. Nina answered the door.

Poppy August stood in the hallway. "May I?"

"Sure," Nina said. She let the younger woman in. "Go smoke outside, Steve."

Dane nodded and went out. Nina shut the door behind him but did not throw the lock. He wandered down the hall, turned right, and found a doorway leading to an outside walkway that stretched along the length of the mansion. He leaned on the flat top of the stone wall. The water, black as night, whispered with the wind. Helsinki winked in the distance.

What did Poppy want this time? Had Savelev told her something?

Dane put the questions out of his mind and smoked.

Footsteps behind him.

He exhaled smoke and turned around.

Sean McFadden stood at the corner. "Hello."

Dane said, "I wondered when you'd show up."

McFadden joined Dane at the wall.

"Enjoy dinner?"

"What did you tell her, Sean?"

"Nothing yet. She asked me to check you out, so I suppose I have until tomorrow. You've put me in a bloody tough spot."

"I was right then."

"About what?"

"If you meant to do me in, you'd have told her."

"Are we going to keep playing this game? You can't win. It's just the two of you. The Duchess has twenty men here. It doesn't matter where you hide or if you use one of the boats to escape."

Dane smoked his cigar.

"I always admired your confidence," McFadden said. "You could look a starving lion in the eye and shrug it off. You always delivered on that. I also saw you blink once or twice. How much of that confidence is an act?"

Dane smiled and smoked his cigar.

"I don't want to kill you," McFadden said. "There's a bond between us whether I want to admit it or not. I also have my client to think about. You know how it is."

"You're all heart."

"The boats are fully fueled. Nobody will notice if you decide to leave in the middle of the night."

Dane puffed on his cigar.

"Are you listening to me?"

"I'm not leaving, Sean."

McFadden inhaled a deep breath and let it out slowly. "Fine. Good luck. I guess you're going to need it."

"I guess."

"You have until daylight."

"Copy that."

"You're a fool."

"Come with us."

"That again?"

"Last chance."

"Same to you. Be gone by daybreak, or else."

McFadden turned and walked away. Dane finished his cigar and rejoined Nina.

She said, "Poppy wanted to know how long till we busted out of here. Alek is pushing for them to run off together."

Dane ignored the update and told her of his exchange with McFadden.

"How long before McConn gets here?" she said.

"I don't know." Dane hauled out the carrying case that contained his other pistol and checked it. He slung the Detonics under his right arm.

Dane cracked open the window and listened. No sign of any choppers. No other noises disturbed the night. Movement in the courtyard caught his attention. Two figures moved toward the door of a bungalow detached from the main building. The Duchess and Alek Savelev. They spoke for a few minutes, and then Savelev turned and walked away while the Duchess entered the bungalow and closed the door. Lights snapped on inside.

Dane looked over at Nina, who was checking her own gun and loading spare magazines. He watched as her thin fingers pushed the rounds into each clip.

"We'll wait three hours," he said, "then you grab Poppy and make for the boats. I'll join you if I can."

"What do you mean if?"

"I can't have Sean nipping at my heels. One way or another, this ends tonight."

Chapter Forty-Eight

Nina snored on the bed while Dane sat beneath the still-open window, his legs out in front of him. Only the night sounds reached his ears, the rustle of trees in the 1 a.m. breeze and the lapping of the water beyond.

He knew McFadden's strengths and weaknesses better than anybody. McFadden knew his. But this would not be an even match. Sean would have, if he'd been telling the truth, plenty of men behind him.

None of those troops were in evidence, other than the two guards they'd seen, but that did not mean they were figments of the Irishman's imagination. It was a large property.

Dane's phone beeped.

He looked at the display and sat up.

Coming in hot be ready.

Dane woke Nina. As she wiped sleep from her eyes, a Klaxon horn began to blare.

So much for surprise.

Dane and Nina raced out to the walkway. The Klaxon continued to wail. Automatic weapons fire crackled. The shots joined the roaring rotor blades of Blackhawk helicopters above. Dane couldn't hear his own footsteps.

Dane drew the Scoremaster and told Nina, "Get Poppy," before he leapt over the wall and dropped to the courtyard below. His feet smacked the ground, and he winced as jolts of fire flashed up his legs. He ran for the bungalow, stumbled a little, but corrected his stride halfway across the courtyard. Lights came on inside the bungalow. Dane kicked open the door, which slammed against the opposing wall and started to swing back. Dane put out his free hand to block the door while raising the .45. The Duchess, armed with a pistol, hesitated to fire at him; when bullets tore chunks out of the doorframe, spitting bits of wood at Dane's face, he turned, dropping into a crouch, and fired back at McFadden as his former ally dashed for cover. Dane pivoted back to face the Duchess, blasting at her as she made a run for sliding glass doors. The Detonics locked open. She fired twice in return and slipped out.

Dane reloaded and turned around again as Sean broke cover. Dane raised his gun.

"You can't win, Dane!"

"Seems I have a little help!"

A new voice added: "More than a little!"

Dane and McFadden watched Nina and Poppy approach, both aiming at McFadden. Sean looked at Dane and grinned.

"Now's your chance to get away, Sean."

"Dane, you simply don't get it."

Another figure arrived. Savelev. "Where's Angelica? What's going on?"

"Why don't you have a gun, Alek?"

"Sean, what—" Alek took in the standoff with quick and nervous glances. He indeed had no gun. McFadden took out his spare and tossed it at him. Savelev caught the pistol clumsily. "Who do I point it at?"

"All three," McFadden said. "They've been playing you the whole time."

Savelev turned shocked eyes on Nina and Poppy. "Poppy?"

"I'm not going away with you," the redhead said.

Savelev turned the gun on Poppy but Nina fired first, stitching three rounds across the Russian's chest. As he fell, a chopper roared overhead with a fiery contrail zeroing in on its backside. The missile struck and the Blackhawk exploded, the fireball lighting up the night, and the flaming hulk of the remains smashed through the main building with a thunderous crash. The ground shook. More searing flames erupted, driving everybody in the courtyard to cover.

Nina and Poppy regrouped with Dane as Sean bolted for the southern point of the island. For the boats tied there.

Dane eyed the wreckage in the burning building and wondered who had been aboard. The heat was too much, singeing his skin, and it could not have been any better for the two women.

"Come on."

He hustled in the direction McFadden had gone, herding Nina and Poppy before him. "Head for the boats."

Not only was it a chance to catch McFadden and maybe the Duchess, but the route would lead them away from the rest of the fighting.

The remaining Blackhawks continued passing overhead. Commandos in black, like falling spiders, zip-lined to the ground. Crackling automatic weapons punctuated by explosions continued at a rapid pace. Dane, Nina and Poppy followed a sloping stone path. It ended abruptly ahead, and a black nothingness took its place. Had Dane not known better, it would have been a frightening sight. The end of the earth. The glow of the fire behind them lit the way, and Dane, gun in hand, scanned the flickering and shifting shadows for any threat. Low tree branches whipped his face. He bent his body to avoid them. Nina bolted right, Poppy following, as he led them off the path and onto the jetty where the boats waited.

The first slip was empty, the mooring lines floating on the water's surface. Poppy jumped into the next boat and stood waiting while Nina raced to the driver's seat. Dane untied the ropes. The boat started to drift from the jetty. Dane leapt aboard, rocking the boat as his shoes slammed onto the bottom, Poppy grabbing for a grip. Nina fired up the engine. Pushing the throttle forward, she steered away from the island and into the dark abyss.

Nina said, "How far to Helsinki?"

"I don't know, but they'll be going flat out so—"

Poppy shouted, "Behind us!"

Dane left Nina's side and rejoined Poppy at the stern. The other boat, closing fast, moved in a zigzag that, along with the choppy water, made it a horrible target. But it wouldn't help McFadden either, who sat at the bow with an assault rifle while the Duchess steered.

"Punch it!" Dane shouted. Nina increased the throttle.

Poppy steadied the little Glock in both hands and started firing. Dane fired the .45, trying to match the shots with the zigzagging boat. The Duchess straightened her course as they came within range, and McFadden opened up with the automatic rifle.

The flashing muzzle spat a salvo, and the slugs cut through the air. Dane returned fire as McFadden corrected his aim. His next blast strafed one side of the boat. Dane and Poppy fired again and again.

Chapter Forty-Nine

The other boat dropped back. Poppy kept shooting, but Dane told her to save her ammo. The Detonics was empty, and Dane used the lull to slap in another magazine. His last.

The Duchess swung wide across the gulf, and Dane squatted down and told Poppy to get low too. The Duchess steered back toward them, cutting across their wake, McFadden firing two quick bursts.

Nina yelped. Dane looked back. One of the slugs had struck her console, but she wasn't hurt. Poppy fired twice as the Duchess closed in, and McFadden's rifle spat more fire. The slugs came nowhere near.

This was getting them nowhere. Dane glanced at a passing island and told Nina to turn for it. She cut across the water and slowed as she stopped perpendicular to the island in a muddy cove. Nina jumped out first, splashing across the shallow water. Dane grabbed Poppy's arm and yanked her out.

The Duchess and McFadden closed in, and McFadden let a long burst go. The rounds smacked into the earth and foliage. Poppy screamed as she fell forward, Dane losing his grip. Her right foot was stuck in the wet mud. She hauled her foot out, minus the shoe, and started running again. McFadden took aim and fired. The rounds struck Poppy with a wet slap, and she fell again. This time she did not get up.

Dane fired back as McFadden and the Duchess exited the boat. McFadden sprayed covering fire while the Duchess dove into the foliage. She had no weapon but wore something across her chest. A satchel. What was inside?

"Come on, Steve!"

With a grunt he followed Nina, and they ventured deeper inland.

They had the advantage and disadvantage of the cloudy night and the terrain. The moon was bright but hardly illuminated the battleground. Dane and Nina, separated now, hid amongst the foliage.

His eyes adjusted to the dark, but the odd shapes of trees and plant life and their blending shadows made it hard to make out any intruding forms. McFadden could work the environment to his advantage. Could the Duchess?

Dane didn't look directly at anything but allowed his more sensitive peripheral vision to pick out the odd ducks in the foliage. Something crawled across his left hand. The insects were as unused to him as he was to them, but at least they weren't carrying automatic weapons.

An explosion lit the darkness, shaking the ground beneath him, the blinding flash stinging his eyes. To the right of his position. Maybe 30 yards away. Bits of shrapnel cut through leaves and peppered the ground around him. A blast of automatic fire followed. McFadden and the Duchess had no idea where he and Nina were hiding, but now he knew they also had grenades. That's what was in the

Duchess's satchel! They were trying to smoke them out. Dane didn't move. The worst thing he could do was break cover. The only thing he could do was keep his eyes open and his trigger finger ready.

Another explosion and another blast of automatic weapons fire. Twenty yards. No shrapnel this time. Closer, but Dane still did not move. He let his eyes do the hunting. If they were close, they were moving, and if they were moving, they would show themselves. McFadden had always been an anxious fighter. The lack of feedback from the grenade blasts would lull him into a false sense of security. It had happened before, more than once. Dane didn't think he'd learned to take things slowly in the time they had been apart.

He heard the next grenade sail overhead, nicking branches as it flew. He buried his face in the wet dirt. The blast came from behind. The heat of the flames burned his neck. Sharp bits of metal tugged at his clothing. Closer. Dane looked up and around and spotted a human figure rising from a crouch. The figure was joined by another, and the pair stepped around the natural obstacles. The figure in front pointed a weapon off to Dane's right and fired a short burst.

Two quick replies from Nina's S&W answered the burst, but neither target fell. The masculine of the two forms fired a longer burst in return, while the feminine figure pulled the pin on another grenade. *Now!* Dane fired four rounds in quick succession. The figure with the raised arm fell. The other screamed. Dane shut his eyes and buried his face in the ground. The grenade detonated, and the explosion might as well have shaken the world's foundation.

Dane raised his head, waiting, his nerves an inferno of their own.

Minutes ticked by.

"Nina!"

"I'm okay!"

Dane wiped his face and scrambled from position, his clothes and hands covered in mud. He approached the site of the blast. Some of the foliage had caught fire and quietly burned.

Nina crunched through the undergrowth and stopped beside him. They found the Duchess first, her remains scattered across several feet but the bulk of her body recognizable.

Dane found the other ripped and charred body a few steps away. It lay on one side. Dane used a foot to roll McFadden onto his back. McFadden's dying eyes found his. McFadden made a sound through puffy lips. Dane knelt down and leaned close.

"It didn't have to be this way," Dane said.

"No other way," McFadden whispered. His words seemed to come from far away, a place Dane couldn't reach. "Finish it."

"Okay." Dane stood up and lifted his gun. McFadden's eyes did not leave his. Dane squeezed the trigger.

The echo of the shot faded fast, but Dane stood there a long time looking at the dead man. Nina tugged on his arm. Time to go.

Chapter Fifty

Dane and Nina, with Poppy's body, took the boat back to the island.

Dane stood up front beside Nina, who steered the boat, her eyes set forward, her face still. Dane tried to ignore the rough bumps as the boat sped along.

He put a hand on Nina's shoulder.

"I'm sorry about Alek."

She touched his hand with her left. "I'm sorry about Sean."

Dane kissed her cheek and moved to the back of the boat. He sat next to Poppy's body. It bounced and flopped with every jolt. He'd never liked the girl, but she had deserved better. The cycle of life once again had interrupted with its own agenda. One day you were consumed with the circumstances and problems of the living, the next you joined the ranks of the dead. No ceremony and no good-bye and no time to process the transition. Back to the ashes from which you'd been made, your final act only to settle debts with your Creator. Who knew what happened after that? If there was life after death, Dane hoped Poppy August reached a peaceful destination. But would she still be Poppy August when she arrived? If not, he didn't want to know.

Nina held steady at the wheel and steered toward the mansion. Fires still burned, but as they drew closer, Dane no longer heard the crackles of combat.

Dane went to Nina's side, holding her as she steered. She did not resist. They needed the rest she had talked about in Mexico and Steve Dane vowed they would have it. Thankfully, they would have it together.

Nina docked and cut the motor. Dane lifted Poppy's body over his shoulders.

They reached the courtyard, where a group of armed men in combat fatigues ordered them to stop and surrender.

"We're the good guys!" Dane shouted. And then two men stepped forward, pulling off the balaclava masks that concealed their faces.

McConn and Lukavina.

"Lower your weapons," Lukavina ordered. "They're ours."

Days later, in the quiet confines of a Helsinki hotel, Steve Dane sat on the edge of the bed and lifted the handset of the night-stand telephone.

He dialed a number from memory and waited for the connection. Bandages concealed by his clothes covered his body, but the injuries would heal quickly. The emotional scars, he knew, required more time. But he had the time. He intended to fully take advantage of it.

The other end of the line picked up and a man answered curtly.

Dane identified himself, adding: "If the President is awake, I need to talk to him."

"Wait one."

A moment passed. "Hello?"

"It's me, sir."

"Stephen! I cannot tell you how glad I am to hear your voice."

"It's been a long time, Mr. President."

"Yes, it has."

"I suppose you heard about a certain recording."

"I have."

"It's taken care of."

"Are you okay?"

"We'll be fine. How are you?"

"Very well, Stephen."

Silence. Dane listened to his own breathing and that of the other man.

The President said, "I light a candle for you every day."

"I believe you."

Dane closed his eyes. His pulse pounded in his head; the heartbeat in his chest felt like a jackhammer cutting through rock.

"I'll be here when you're ready to come home."

"I know."

"We can't lose you."

"I'm not lost, sir. Only adrift."

"Where are you going next?"

"Home, probably."

"Your home is *here*, Stephen."

Dane shut his eyes tight. There was no use in talking any further.

"Good-bye, Peter."

The other man did not hang up or say good-bye. Dane let the silence linger, the hum of the line the only connection between the two of them. Between a past Dane could not run from forever and the present. Someday there would be no choice. He would face the circumstances that had put him on his present course. But that day was not today. The ghosts of battles past would wait for him in his dreams; for now, that was the only place he wanted to see them.

Dane slowly cradled the receiver and sat for a long time, staring at the carpet.

After a while, he stepped out onto the balcony, where Nina and Todd waited. The loose ends were still being tied up. The Finnish had to be soothed. That was up to the diplomats. Dane had given Lukavina the location of the M5205, and his friend would get credit for its recovery. Other than that, Dane wasn't concerned with the rest.

McConn handed him a drink, and Dane lit a cigar. The three of them looked out on the view of Helsinki, and nobody said a word. For now, the company of his friends was all that Dane required.

Nina exited the bathroom with a towel wrapped around her body and head. She stopped short. Dane remained on the balcony, alone, staring into space. McConn had been gone about an hour, and she'd figured he'd come inside and watch television while she showered, but the way he stared communicated that something was on his mind that neither she nor McConn had been able to decipher.

She traded the towel for a robe and tied the belt around her waist. The soft terrycloth felt wonderful against her naked skin.

He turned as she opened the sliding glass door and stepped onto the deck.

"You'll catch a cold," he said.

"Don't worry about me."

"You're wondering why I'm still standing out here."

"What did you and Cross talk about?"

"Home."

"And?"

"It's not time to go back yet."

"When will it be? You can't run forever."

"I'm not running."

"You're afraid," she said.

"Of what?"

"That the rumors are true. That your father betrayed the United States. That he wasn't framed, despite what you think. That the reason Cross couldn't help when you worked for him at CIA as because there wasn't anything he could do. There wasn't somebody else responsible."

Dane looked away. They heard a commotion a few balconies away. Laughter. A party.

"If my father hadn't killed himself," Dane said, "maybe we'd know more."

Nina said, "There's only one way to find out. You have to go back."

"What if I really am afraid?" he said.

"Then we keep moving until you aren't anymore."

Finally, he looked at her, but his expression remained too stoic to read.

"Come to bed," she said, tugging on his shirt.

The party sounds increased, only to be presently joined by a sound more dreadful than the wailing of souls from the seventh circle of Hell.

"I don't believe it," she said.

Dane groaned.

"Did he follow us here?" she said.

"I'm sure it's a coincidence."

The accordion player from Venice, the tune from his instrument as loud and obnoxious as ever, played to the party crowd, the terrible noise echoing into the night.

"What is it with this guy and polka?" Dane said.

"I'm not feeling amorous anymore," Nina said. "What do you intend to do about this while I put on my flannel pajamas?"

"Well—"

"You promised you'd smash his skull. Did you lie to me in Mexico?"

"Well—"

"Do I need to remind you—"

"All right, all right. Step aside please."

She moved a step to the left, and he passed through the balcony door.

"What are you going to do?" she said.

"I'll smack his other eye this time."

Nina let out a delightful squeal. "I'm getting aroused again!" she announced.

He reached the door and said, "Be naked when I get back."

Nina laughed.

A Look At:
Another Way To Kill: A Steve Dane Thriller

Monaco was a nice vacation—until Steve Dane and Nina Talikova witness a secret agent's murder.

They are now loose ends in a Russian conspiracy to steal a direct-energy weapon from the U.S., but the assassins pursuing them have made a grave miscalculation. Dane and Nina are former spies who know all the tricks and invented a few themselves. Their trail of vengeance leads from Monaco to Texas to a showdown in the Gulf of Mexico, where Dane is taken prisoner by an opponent who intends to settle old hatreds long thought buried.

Outgunned and alone, Steve Dane doesn't soft-sell his brand of payback. He negotiates the only terms the enemy understands: certain death.

AVAILABLE JULY 2021

Made in the USA
Las Vegas, NV
11 June 2023

73293607R00163